THE EYE OF CALLANISH

Books by Moyra Caldecott

FICTION
Guardians of the Tall Stones:
The Tall Stones
The Temple of the Sun
Shadow on the Stones
The Silver Vortex

Weapons of the Wolfhound
The Eye of Callanish
The Lily and the Bull
The Tower and the Emerald
Etheldreda
Child of the Dark Star
Hatshepsut: Daughter of Amun
Akhenaten: Son of the Sun
Tutankhamun and the Daughter of Ra
The Ghost of Akhenaten
The Winged Man
The Waters of Sul
The Green Lady and the King of Shadows

NON-FICTION/MYTHS AND LEGENDS
Crystal Legends
Three Celtic Tales
Women in Celtic Myth
Myths of the Sacred Tree
Mythical Journeys: Legendary Quests

CHILDREN'S STORIES
Adventures by Leaflight

THE EYE OF CALLANISH

by

Moyra Caldecott

Published by
Bladud Books

First published in a digital edition in 2001
by Mushroom eBooks, an imprint of Mushroom Publishing

This edition published in 2005 by
Bladud Books, an imprint of
Mushroom Publishing, Bath, UK

www.mushroompublishing.com

Cover illustration © Helen Folkes

ISBN 1-84319-120-2

Printed and Bound by
Lightning Source

Contents

Introduction

This story is set at the beginning of the twelfth century on the Island of Lewis in the Outer Hebrides, off the west coast of Scotland.

A young girl, persecuted for being in league with the Devil, believes herself to be psychically in touch with the ancient people who built the temple of Tall Stones at Callanish.

There is a suggestion in the story that these people might have come from the West, the legendary land Saint Brendan had sailed to in the sixth century, the Vinland of the Vikings, and North America of the present day. Amerindian legends of ancient migrations and recent archaeological excavations of earth works, quoits and underground chambers in North America give support to this suggestion, as does the similarity in concept between the Amerindian Medicine Wheel and the ancient Stone Circles of Britain. Yachtsmen have told me that it is easier to sail across the northern Atlantic ocean from west to east than it is from east to west. I am not suggesting however that the American Indians as we know them today emigrated to Britain, but that some ancient people – the forerunners of us both – *may* have. Callanish itself has a legend of people coming from over the sea in ships, landing, building the temple, the priests wearing tall feathered head dresses and feathered cloaks with wrens and sacred birds circling above their heads.

This theme however is only one thread in a story that is mostly concerned with the strange human phenomenon of being at once fascinated by the search for Truth . . . and terrified of it . . .

The story also follows the further adventures of Neil, who was the hero of *Weapons of the Wolfhound*, and the hermit Durston, who, it was suggested in that book, carved the magnificent walrus ivory chess pieces known as the Lewis chess set now in the British Museum, London.

'O God, kindle in my heart
A glimmer of the sun's warmth towards my neighbour,
Towards my enemy, towards my kindred, towards my
friend,
Towards the free, towards the slave, towards the
bondsman -
O Sons of the Earth soft and fair,
From the lowest created thing
Up to the Circle Most High.'

Ancient Gaelic prayer offered at the time of the lighting of
the Bealltuinn fires on May Day.
Quoted on p.154 of *The Islands of Western Scotland* by
W.H.Murray, Eyre Methuen, 1973, from *History of Skye* by
A. Nicolson, 1930.

Chapter 1

The Journey

The marshlands were full of waterfowl at this time of year, and sometimes it seemed to Neil that their island was more suitable for these creatures than it was for humans. So much water reflected the blue of the sky that his horse's hooves often seemed to wade through clouds at the edges of the meres.

It was a good day to start on a journey . . . a good day to be alive. He sang. The birds sang. The clouds scudded above and below and a cool, clean breeze lifted the silky threads of the bog-cotton and set them drifting to far away places.

The rumour that there was a pure white mare for sale in the village of Kirkoway on the eastern shores of Loch Roag, of exactly the kind Fiona, his sister, had set her heart on, had reached their farm only two days before. Neil's father, Lorn, had at first intended to fetch it himself, but had found that he was too busy. So Neil was chosen as the best horseman of the family to ride to Kirkoway. He was delighted to leave behind his daily chores and to ride out into the world.

'I will never be a contented farmer,' he thought, the hills riding beside him, reflected in the mirror-smooth pools.

When he was a young boy he had run away to Iceland with a Viking sea captain called Baldur, and had returned home exhausted after Baldur's death, satiated with dangerous adventures and only too glad to settle down to the quiet of his father's farm. He had sat at the feet of Durston, the hermit who lived on the headland near his home, and tried to learn everything he was prepared to teach. He remembered how he had contrasted the active, violent life of the Viking, moving from one place to another as though the moving was an end in itself – with the quiet, contemplative life of the hermit, deeply aware of the rich adventures available to the spirit while the body remained in one place.

Neil remembered how he had said he was sick of the farm and the Island.

'There is nothing here but wind and water and sheep and cows!' he had grumbled.

Durston had smiled quizzically and replied: 'Have you not seen the lichen and moss more beautiful than the finest tapestries in the royal palaces – heather crisper and richer than the thickest carpet – butterwort and flowering cotton grass, bog asphodel and lily clad more grandly than the finest ladies? Have you not seen the cunning sundew outwitting the dragonfly? Have you not seen the marshland and the green coastal hills teeming with birds: the winchat, the whitethroat, the neat sandpiper, the agile dipper turning pebbles over at the bottom of clear running streams? Have you not seen the rocky crags, castles of the golden eagle, the merlin and the buzzard? What sickness has blinded you to the beautiful golden plover, the blue-black raven, the red grouse and the courageous storm petrel? The thickets are teeming with animals: the otter, the hare, the red deer . . . The rivers . . .'

All that Durston had said that day was true – his island world was beautiful, rich, exciting, but nevertheless . . .

Suddenly a bird sprang up from almost under his horse's hooves and hurtled to the sky. Neil's heart stirred. If only he could travel that far and that fast. If only he were not bound by the earth – by flesh and bone . . . He had learned much from Durston and he was not the foolish boy he had once been – but he had never achieved the far and free-ranging spirit the hermit seemed to have. Physical journeys and physical places still called to him.

Digging his heals into his bronze-red stallion he set off at a gallop.

'Go, Flame! Go.' he cried, and as though he too was excited at the thought of freedom, Flame responded to his master's mood

4

and was away over the dark, soft moss and peat, shreds of it flying up from his hooves, his mane streaming out behind his head like the flame he was named for.

Neil's eyes shone, his breath came in short, joyful bursts, his heart pounded with the same rhythm as the hooves. Earth . . . air . . . water . . . and the fire of his horse! All the elements! He was master of all the elements!

Having left at first light on a long summer's day, Neil could have reached Kirkoway before night-fall, but he had no wish to end his journey: he and Flame were enjoying the sense of freedom and the possibility of adventure too much. The wild galloping, alternating with quiet walking and a considerable period of dreaming beside the silver waters of Little Loch Roag meant that when evening approached he was still some distance from his destination. On the near shore of Loch Ceann Hulavig he found a fisherman who gave him shelter for the night and shared his meal of fish and ale. They sat for a long while beside the quiet water exchanging stories while the colour of the sky gradually deepened into purple and then into black, and the peninsulas and islands of the sea-loch gradually disappeared in the shadows. The man remembered how he had escaped to the sea when the fierce Norwegian king, Magnus Bareleg, had devastated the Island with fire, destroying every last tree and most of its people. Neil knew that his own father, as a young child, had narrowly escaped death at this time, though he never talked about it. To Lorn the important things in life were the slow rhythm of the seasons, the growth of crops from seed to harvest, and the love of his family. Wars might come and go and so might storms. He weathered both as best he could and lived his own life his own way in spite of them. But the fisherman was a born storyteller, and before it became too dark to see he pointed out to Neil all the hills that had been covered with trees before the Norsemen had set torch to them. And he described with relish the screams he had heard before he had pulled away from the shore, the terrible scenes on the beach as too many people, frantic with fear, had tried to clamber into the few little fishing coracles, and how he had had to push them away, clubbing a woman because she would not let go of the edge of the boat when it was already over-loaded.

Neil shivered and looked up at the immense dark sky above them, seeded with stars. He hoped such power over life and death would never be in his gift.

The fisherman gave a great yawn at last and said that he was going to sleep. Neil paused at the low door and took one last deep breath of fresh air before he entered the man's dark hovel, and cast one last awed look over his shoulder at the vast heavens. Suddenly it seemed to him that one of the stars detached itself from its fixed and ancient place and crossed the sky. It happened so quickly and was so soon over that Neil was not sure it had happened at all. A slight chill ran through his limbs. Stars were so much a part of the eternal changeless background to man's ephemeral life it made him uneasy to think that they too were temporary and could fall from the sky as easily as apples from a tree.

He lay awake a long time on the rug the fisherman had flung on the floor for him, listening to the sound of the old man's breathing as he wallowed deeply in sleep. At last he drifted off himself. Wherever he stepped in his dream there was water, and in every sheet of water was the reflection of a star falling.

As the night progressed he began to feel more and more uneasy as though the star falling was a warning in some way that he should not take his own bright and easy life too much for granted. He woke depressed and was not surprised to find the sun had gone and that heavy grey clouds hung low and obscured the hills. By the time he came to take his leave the wind had brought a steady driving rain. He unstrapped his sheepskin jerkin from Flame's back and put it on, thinking ruefully back to the warm and golden sunlight of the day before. He wished now that he had hurried and been well under cover at Kirkoway.

He thought about his sister, not much more than a year older than himself, and yet about to be married. The year before a party of young noblemen from the Scottish court had been on the Isle of Lewis, guests of the Norse jarl at Stornoway. Some of them had ridden west – one in particular, Sir Kenneth, from a local family, seeking childhood memories though his own parents were long since dead and he had lived most of his life on the mainland. Neil's parents had made them welcome and Sir Kenneth, the nicest and least Normanized among them, had paid particular attention to his sister. Just before leaving he had asked for her in marriage, but her father had said that the romance was too sudden and that he must wait a year. Messages had gone back and forth, the last announcing that Sir Kenneth would be with them by the end of June, hoping that Fiona's family would now accept him as bridegroom.

It was now very nearly the end of June and Sir Kenneth was on his way to Uig. It was so that his sister would have a worthy steed on which to accompany her new husband that Neil was on his way to Kirkoway. They had been told that the 'sheen of the mare's coat would make the silk of a bishop's cope seen dull'. Neil smiled, in spite of the rain, to think of his tall, beautiful sister with her flame-red hair riding such a steed to meet her new lord. They would show these Mainlanders that islanders could match them elegance for elegance. He smiled also as he remembered his father's anxious and often repeated warnings not to be cheated in the bargaining – to pay a fair price but no more.

What with the rain driving into his face so that he kept his eyes half closed, and his thoughts wandering far and wide, Neil did not realize that he had left the main road until he began to notice that the path was unexpectedly rough and pitted and so narrow that the heather bushes had almost closed over it. Flame startled and almost threw him as his hoof caught in a hidden pot-hole.

Puzzled Neil reined Flame in and looked around. He was beneath a sombre hill which loomed out of the swirling mist, crowned by a clustered group of tall, sinister shapes. His heart skipped a beat.

He had heard of this place. The Norsemen called the hilly peninsula 'Callanish': but the locals always referred to the Standing Stones as the 'Devil's Stones'.

He shuddered. The wind howled, the icy rain stabbed at his skin, and yet, fascinated, he could not leave. He remembered stories he had heard about the Stones . . . how someone who had dared to walk the avenue that led to the central circle had gone mad . . . how a child had disappeared in the district and the villagers had been convinced that it had been taken by the 'Stones'. . .

Neil crossed himself, murmuring a prayer to his god for protection.

'Flame,' he whispered, 'we must get away from here.' But Flame had discovered that there was something to crop after all in this desolate landscape and was happily tugging at the fine grass between the heather and the sedges.

'Flame!' Neil repeated, louder, his voice sounding strange to him as he looked back fearfully at the hilltop.

A shadow moved. *Something* was moving amongst the Stones!

Neil broke out in a sweat.

'Flame!' he shouted, and drove his heels savagely into his peacefully cropping steed. The horse reared in protest, whinnying loudly, and Neil was flung off his back onto the rough, wet ground.

'O Lord save me!' he almost sobbed, convinced that the Devil would surely have him now. Flame moved off unconcerned, and left his master struggling with slippery clinging heather branches and mud that sucked at his feet. He dragged himself upright at last and ran stumbling towards his horse. Flame was cropping again a little distance away – sensing no harmful influences.

Twice Neil fell as he ran towards him and twice missed his grip on Flame's wet back as he tried to mount. Convinced that there was some dire spirit trying to hold him back he was shivering with fear. But at last – muddy, dishevelled and shaken he was mounted and, without a backward glance, was galloping back across the headland towards the main road from which he had so foolishly strayed.

Behind him, though he did not see it, the mist was lifting and the sun was touching the stones so that they shone like silver at the top of the hill. A young girl standing among them detached herself and mounted a white mare.

She did not follow him, but picked her way carefully down the other side of the slope, towards the shimmering sea.

Chapter 2

The Nocturnal Ride

By the time he reached Kirkoway, Neil had recovered his composure. But just in case there was any lingering shadow of influence from the weird Stones, he tethered Flame and went into the tiny grey church that stood on the hill overlooking the village. He knelt on the cold stone floor in the dim interior and prayed for protection from evil spirits. The figure of the dead Christ hanging from a cross overshadowed the whole place. The silence was heavy and he was as glad to leave this place as he had been to leave the Devil's Stones.

Outside he found Flame surrounded by interested children, nervously and shyly stamping and tossing his head, not sure whether to trust the many small hands that were stroking and pulling at his mane and tail. Neil took his bridle and led him away, the children excitedly accompanying him, only too happy to point out the house where the owner of the white horse lived.

It was a woman who greeted Neil when the children shouted at the door, and when she heard that he was interested in buying the white mare she apologized for her husband not being at home and invited him in. The children tried to crowd in after them, but she chased them away with a show of fierceness. They scattered, laughing and chattering, eager to spread the news of the arrival of a stranger in the village: a stranger who asked about the white mare.

The woman looked older than she was. Her face was tired and sad and as she moved she hunched her shoulder in a way that suggested that she was used to fending off sudden blows. He soon noticed that she was unwilling to talk about the mare and decided to leave the subject until her husband returned. He watched her stirring a huge iron cauldron of mutton broth that hung over the central peat fire, and thought how lucky he was to live in a house with many rooms. The steam was rising into the thatch and the smell pervaded the whole cottage.

He established that her husband was a freeman with a small-holding of arable land and grazing for four animals, unlike the other villagers who were mostly fishermen. The loch came close in against the hill on which the church stood, to make a fine sheltered harbour. The couple had one daughter, but the woman seemed as unwilling to talk about her as she was to talk about the white mare.

Neil began to wonder how such people could own a Norman horse? Even the tough, stocky little Island horses were almost unknown in villages as small as this, but a horse bred from the stock the Normans had brought from France would be very rare indeed. Such animals were usually only to be found belonging to one of the great Norse lords or a family such as his own – descended from a chief's family and the daughter of a Norse jarl.

Neil was beginning to be impatient with the long wait when he heard the clatter of hooves outside. As he moved to the door to see who it was, he fancied the woman gave him an anxious look, but he soon forgot her completely as his eyes took in the scene in front of the house. The heavy grey clouds that had hung over him during most of his journey that morning had lifted and a shaft of light illumined the white mare and its rider. Nothing he had heard had prepared him for what he saw. The steed was quicksilver and moonlight, the rider a young woman of extraordinary beauty, slender and graceful, hair of midnight and eyes of midday. The two, rider and mount, were so perfectly in harmony with each other that Neil knew then, in his heart, that he could not bear to separate them.

He heard the woman move behind him and felt her push him aside as she came to stand at the door.

'Where have you been?' she cried, and her voice was both angry and frightened.

The young woman looked at her mother and then, without answering, looked back at Neil. He felt awkward, clumsy, and as though he owed her some kind of explanation.

He stepped forward, but found that he could think of nothing to say. Her gaze did not waver. Whether she had heard what he had come for or not he could not tell. Her eyes were wary, but not hostile. He walked over to her and touched the white mare's nose. Nervously she twitched away from his hand. The girl murmured something and stroked her ears reassuringly.

'She's beautiful,' he said at last. 'What do you call her?'

For a long while the girl sat perfectly still, staring at the mare's silver mane. Her mother had gone back into the house and they were alone in a cocoon of silence which separated them from the rest of the world.

'She's called Moon-Metal,' she said at last in a very low voice, 'because . . .' And then she paused.

'Because?' he prompted.

'Because she came to me at full moon . . . shining like silver.'

He was puzzled by this, but not surprised that the mare had come into the family by extraordinary means.

'And your name?' he asked gently.

'Mairi,' she said simply. The way she said it reminded him of a song he had heard as a child – a song left over from the days when the fires were lit regularly on the beacon hills.

They heard a rough voice shouting and looked round to see a huge, thickset man with a red face bearing down on them.

'My father,' Mairi said quickly, and all the light seemed to go out of her face. Without a word of greeting to him she touched Moon-Metal's flanks with her heels and walked her away round the side of the cottage.

Neil found it difficult to believe that Mairi was the daughter of this uncouth giant and the faded wisp of a woman in the cottage. She might have had something of the cast of her mother's features perhaps . . . for there was still some evidence left in that tired face that the woman had once been beautiful . . . but there was nothing of her father in her, and it would seem by the haste with which she had left at his approach there was no great affection between them.

'You have come to see the mare,' the man growled as soon as he was near enough. His eyes were deeply suspicious and there was no welcoming smile on his lips.

'I have,' Neil said quickly. 'I heard that she was for sale. But if that is not true . . .'

'Who said it was not true?' snapped the man. 'If the price is right . . .'

'Your daughter seems very fond of her. I would not want to . . .'

'My daughter has no say in the matter!' the man said sharply. 'The mare is for sale.'

Neil was silent. He wished that his family had never heard of the white mare.

'Perhaps . . . if I had some idea of what you considered a fair price . . .'

'All in good time,' Mairi's father said, his harsh voice softening a little. 'Do I speak to a man without a name?'

Neil told him his name and his father's name, and his grandfather's name.

'From Uig . . . from beyond the high peaks?'

'Yes.' He was glad his family was recognised. It would make it more unlikely that he would be cheated.

'You have come a long way, second son of Lorn.'

'The fame of the white mare has spread a long way.'

The man's eyes narrowed. He looked hard at Neil.

'What have you heard?'

'Of her beauty . . . of her speed . . . that she is descended from a Saracen horse brought back by the Normans from the holy crusade.'

'And that is all?'

'Is there more?'

The man was silent, his face closed and thoughtful.

'No,' he said at last. 'There is no more.'

* * * *

14

Neil did not see Mairi in the afternoon. She sat silently with them while they drank some of her mother's unappetizing broth and ate some flat, sour bread, but disappeared as soon as she had cleared away the bowls and platters.

Her father, Braden, insisted on showing him the white mare himself. Neil noticed that she was ill at ease when handled by the man and shied away nervously, but seemed calmer with himself. Braden pulled heavily on the bit and spoke to her roughly. To spare her suffering Neil asked to ride her and was grudgingly given permission. As he rode through the village he dreaded meeting Mairi, wishing that he could speak with her about the mare before he was forced to make a final decision.

It struck him as he rode about that this was one of the most unfriendly villages he had ever visited. Everyone he met stared at him, but no one greeted him. If he smiled and waved they were prepared to nod in response, but none chose to speak to him or to welcome him as a stranger should be welcomed. Even the children who had been so friendly before, ran to see him as he passed by, or gathered in groups to stare after him, but there was something in their way of looking at him now that puzzled him. It was as though they were waiting for something to happen.

Once she was over her shyness with him the silver mare was a pleasure to ride. He took her away from the village and galloped her towards the open moorland, glad to be away from the brooding shadow that seemed to hang over the village. The mare had grace and speed and sensitivity. He wished he could ride away home there and then and not have to face the girl's sorrow and the man's greed. He changed his mind several times – at one moment determined to leave the mare with Mairi, at another, coveting the beautiful creature for his sister. He remembered how her eyes had shone so much at the thought of the mare that her family had teased her by asking whom she would cherish more, Sir Kenneth, her bridegroom, or the white mare, her steed.

The sea, now that the light had broken through, was patched with silver, the deep grey water holding innumerable shining mirrors to the sun. From the height of the moor he could see the islands stretching into the distance, while behind him moor-land and marsh lay without feature until they faded into the clouds that still clung to the horizon.

He turned Moon-Metal back and rejoined the cottages that straggled over the hill. Apart from a young lad, who looked up from his hoeing and stared after him with no response to his waving hand, he saw no one. Even the children were elsewhere, probably at their chores, tending the sheep or the few lean cows he had noticed during his ride. Mairi was still nowhere in sight and neither was her father. Her mother, Skena, was spinning some rough black wool at the entrance to the cottage.

That night he was expected to sleep in the empty cattle byre, an extension of the one long room of the house, on a bed of straw and rugs. He had managed to avoid making a commitment one way or another about the mare, and had said he would give his decision in the morning. He knew that Mairi knew now about the purpose of his visit, but she said nothing. She seemed to be surrounded by a very strong but invisible shell which Neil found impossible to penetrate. Whenever he tried to draw her into conversation at the evening meal, one of her parents would answer for her, and she passively allowed them to do this. Once or twice he had the feeling that the shell was all that there was of her at the table, that the rest of her was somewhere else.

Braden talked and talked, grumbling endlessly about the dif-ficulties forcing a livelihood out of the earth, and how he would have managed better if he had sons. Neil looked at Mairi. She had heard this many times before and her face showed no reac-tion. Only her hands moved suddenly, pushing her wooden platter away from her, the food untouched. Neil saw that her hands were working hands. No doubt Braden made sure that she did the work of the sons he did not have even if he refused to give her credit for it.

The uneaten food started a storm which only abated when Neil announced that he was tired and insisted that he be shown where he was to sleep.

He lay in the byre and waited for the family to settle down for the night. All that had happened since he had left home went round and round in his head. He wished he could understand what it was that bothered him about the community in which he had found himself. They seemed to know something that he did not know. The elegance of the mare, and the delicate beauty of the girl did not fit in. She would have been more at home in his family than in hers. Something in the way looks passed between the man and the woman whenever the mare or Mairi were mentioned . . . something in the way the villagers had stared at him . . .

Braden kept stressing the value of the mare and Neil knew that although no price had yet been fixed, it would not be low. 'Perhaps,' he thought, 'perhaps I can tell Fiona that the mare was not for sale – or that the price was too high . . .' But he knew somehow in his heart that he was not going to ride away from Moon-Metal as easily as that. As every moment passed he had felt himself more and more involved in a situation he could not understand, but which he knew he could not leave.

It was as though by coming to this village his destiny had taken a turn and a twist from which there was now no escape.

It was a long time before he drifted off to sleep. His dreams were strange, but when he suddenly jerked awake in the small hours of the morning, he could not remember them. Wide-eyed and listening he strained to catch what it was that had awakened him. Braden was snoring as loudly as the fisherman the night before, and it was impossible to detect any other noise in the cottage. He sat up cautiously, peering into the dark. In the area of the cottage occupied by the family the peat fire was still glowing faintly. Braden gave a particularly loud snort and heaved his great bulk over in bed. The snoring gave way to heavy breathing. Beyond it, outside the cottage, Neil caught the sound that might have woken him. Without hesitation he stood up and crept towards the door. He stooped under the lintel and pulled himself up to his full height outside in the dark. The fresh cold air was sweet, the sky completely clear of clouds, a moon rising.

He caught a flash of movement to the right and, turning towards it, was just in time to see the dim white form of the mare and its rider disappearing behind a hillock.

He ran back to the paddock, found Flame and led him as quietly as he could until he was clear of the village, then he mounted and rode hard in the direction he had seen the white mare take.

The moon was bright and the hills were reasonably well lit. The sheets of water that always lay in the hollows of the rocks shone like ghostly eyes, many catching the moons reflection – giving it back eerily. For a while Neil feared that he had lost the white mare, but he heard a faint whinny in the distance, the sound carrying far in the crisp air and over the empty, treeless landscape. He began to feel uneasy. Mairi was a quiet, secretive person; she would not be pleased to be followed on one of her private night rides. He also began to worry that she was going too far from the village and that they would not be able to get back before the dawn.

He thought of turning back himself and leaving the girl to her solitary ride, possibly the last one she would ever have on her quicksilver steed. But then another thought struck him. What if she was running away with the mare? What if she was going to hide it so that it could not be sold? Once again he was torn between two conflicting emotions: sympathy for her because he too would have wanted to hide the mare if it had been his, and anger that he would now lose the mare for his sister.

He urged Flame to greater recklessness over the shadowed and rocky terrain and tried to lessen the distance between them. He would talk to her and try to explain how loving and careful his sister would be, and what a good life Moon-Metal would have, compared to the cramped conditions of her father's croft. If Mairi did not let her go she would have to endure the winter stabled with pigs and sheep and cows. Her coat would become dull and grimy with the smoke from the cooking fires.

Suddenly Neil rounded a rocky knoll and had a clear view ahead. He drew his breath in sharply and pulled on the reins. In the distance, silhouetted against the skyline, were the Standing

Stones he had encountered the previous day, the Devil Stones – and the girl was riding straight towards them!

He had a bad moment deciding whether to leave her to her fate, or to dare the supernatural dangers himself in order to rescue her. Since he had first seen her she had fascinated him. The very fact that he knew so little about her and that she had been avoiding him drew him after her. Of what could she be thinking to ride so boldly up to that fell place? Was her horse possessed, and she being carried there against her will? At this thought a thrill of fear went through him, but he drove his heels into Flame and rode hard ahead. Even so he was not within reach of the Stones before she had entered the avenue. He could just see her stepping slowly and daintily, leading her silver mare between the tall monoliths.

'Mairi!' he called, but his voice was lost in the huge, hollow night.

He could see her only intermittently, a small white figure leading the white mare, dwarfed by the stones, emerging from the shadows for an instant into the moonlight and then disappearing again.

'Holy angels protect us!' whispered Neil, and dismounted. He would not expose Flame to the danger and left him well back, tethered to a heather bush. He ran, hardly noticing the long, slow hill that he had to climb. At the top he stopped and stared. He was looking straight up the avenue to the circle where the tallest Stone, the one facing the sea and the islands, rose up to the sky. The girl was standing quite still gazing up at it.

Neil could not bring himself to walk up the avenue but he ran beside it until he was near enough to see Mairi quite clearly. The place was extraordinarily still. Moonlight shone on the grey white surfaces of the tall stones. The sea lay peaceful and silver below the headland. He sensed no evil.

The young woman began to walk from stone to stone . . . not as though she were part of some devilish ritual, but as though she were simply enjoying the beauty of the place.

It was clear she had not noticed Neil and, not wanting to intrude, he drew back until he was hidden under the shadow of the small row that led east and west from the central circle. Occasionally she touched a Stone and stood beside it looking up at it thoughtfully. Once she went up to Moon-Metal and laid her cheek against the mare' s neck.

At last she took the reins and led her away, back down the avenue, only mounting up when she was well clear of the tall Stones.

After she had gone Neil stayed a few moments longer. The girl and her horse were well away before he could bring himself to leave, and then, just as he was about to follow her, he was startled by a movement from the shadow at the other side of the east-west arm. A figure detached itself and slipped away down the inland side of the hill.

Neil's heart beat fast. He had not been the only one watching the girl. He hesitated, undecided what to do, and then he moved swiftly forward hoping to catch a better glimpse of whoever it was. Without realising what he was doing he crossed through the circle of Stones and out the other side. No evil befell him. No strange dark shadow took his soul. He saw the other figure for a brief second moving away from the Stones, and then the figure was lost in hill shadow.

He returned to Flame, mounted and rode home. The girl and her white steed were nowhere in sight. As he rode back he noticed nothing of the landscape. His thoughts turned round and round, pondering the scene he had just witnessed.

He reached the village of Kirkoway just before first light and managed to sneak back to his pallett before Braden and his wife awoke. The girl was in her bed, her face turned to the wall, only her tousled black hair showing above the sheepskin blanket. Whether she was awake or not he could not tell.

Chapter 3

The Beast with Many Heads

In the morning Mairi gave no sign that she had been anywhere in the night, nor that she suspected Neil of having followed her. She fed the chickens and cleaned out the byre as quietly as she did every morning, answering her mother in monosyllables when she had to, avoiding speech as much as she could.

Neil did not mention the nocturnal journey either – but watched her with intense interest. She moved with grace – with a light and easy step as though her spirit was not bound down by her life of drudgery.

He thought about her means of escape, the mare that gave her a measure of freedom, and was in a dilemma as to what to do for the best. He hated the thought of leaving her imprisoned in a bleak, harsh lifestyle with a brutal father. On the other hand – would he not be doing her a favour in the long run if he took away the means for her to reach the Devil Stones? What dire influence were they having on her? Would it not be better for her body to be enthralled, than her immortal soul? Besides – how could he go empty handed back to his sister?

He decided to buy the mare.

Braden quoted a price.

Neil said it was too much.

Braden quoted a lower one.

Again Neil refused.

Braden was shocked. He knew the price he was asking was well below what the mare was worth. But he was very anxious to get rid of the creature. He dropped his price again and again it was refused. Braden's face darkened and he looked long and hard at Neil. His lips had become a tight, straight line.

'If you don't want the mare,' he said, 'there are plenty who will willingly take her off my hands.'

'Here?' Neil said scornfully, looking around the village. There was not a man who could afford to pay half the price Braden was asking – let alone a fair price.

'You are not the only stranger to come this way,' Braden said sharply.

'Why am I doing this?' Neil thought. 'I want the mare.' But he knew deep inside he could not take her away from Mairi – no matter what the consequences. She would wither and die like a plant deprived of water and sunlight. 'But it is wrong for her to be so dependent on anything,' he told himself. 'It is wrong for her to . . .'

'What price would you pay?' Braden was asking angrily. Neil shifted from one foot to the other, trying at least to appear as though he were on top of the situation. After a long pause he said something that surprised him as much as it did Braden. 'I have decided against buying.'

'Why?' Braden almost spat the word out.

Neil shrugged his shoulders.

'What have you heard?'

'Nothing,' Neil replied, startled at the vehemence and hostility – maybe even fear – in the man's voice. 'Why? What should I have heard?'

The man controlled himself only with difficulty. Neil could see the struggle in his face.

'There's always talk in this village,' he muttered. 'Not enough work, just talk. One would think that there was nothing to do in the world but talk about other people's business.'

'What did you expect me to hear?'

'Nothing!'

'Well, nothing is what I heard. It was not the talk that changed my mind. I just feel she is not right for my sister. Besides, I don't want to part your daughter from her.' He knew he had made a mistake as soon as he uttered the words. Braden's angry eyes sought the girl who was slopping water out of a wooden bucket into the ditch.

'The sooner that girl is parted from that beast the better – it is yours for whatever you're prepared to pay.'

'Moon-Metal?' Neil cried in surprise.

'Moon-bloody-Metal,' the man snapped. 'Heathen name for a beast who has more truck with the devil than with decent folk.'

'I want no devil horse!' Neil said sharply.

The man's face flushed deep red and a vein stood out on his neck. He turned away and dug savagely into the earth with the hoe. He was as furious with himself now as he was with Neil. He had lost the chance of getting rid of the white mare.

Neil watched him for a while in silence and then turned towards the open fields. Moon-Metal was cropping beside his own horse, Flame.

'Silver and gold,' he thought. 'Ice and fire.'

He strolled over to them, sat on the broad mark-stone at the corner of Braden's field and watched the two for a long time. Wild heather moors and rocks were behind them and the sky, pale and clear, seemed immensely domed above them. He had a feeling of timelessness, as though what was before him would go on forever and there was nothing else in his life but this endless moment sitting on a stone watching this peaceful scene. He did not want to leave this place. There was something here unresolved.

There was a movement beside him and he looked down into the eyes of Mairi. Their blue depths were full of shadows.

'Are you thinking of taking Moon-Metal away from me?' she asked in a low, tense voice. He did not answer immediately and the girl interpreted his silence as affirmation. 'She is not for sale you know,' she added sharply. 'She was a gift. I cannot sell her.'

'Was she a gift to you, or to your father?'

'To me.'

'Then your father has no right to sell her, and unless you want to part with her I could not buy her.'

The girl nodded briefly and turned on her heel. He stared after her disappointed, he felt he had been noble and generous towards her and had hoped that she would respond to this with gratitude. He had expected tears of joy, possibly a warm embrace and kiss, certainly a smile. She gave him none of these things but seemed to take his gesture as her due and regard the decision he had made with such difficulty as the only decision that could possibly have been made.

'Wait!' he called out. She paused, but did not turn round to look at him. Again he had the feeling that it was only her outer shell that waited patiently in front of him, her secret Self was somewhere else. 'I want to talk to you,' he said.

'There is nothing to talk about,' she replied.

He jumped down from the stone. 'There is a great deal to talk about,' he said. 'Why do you turn from me like that? I've told you that I'll not be taking the mare from you if you don't want me to.'

'For that I thank you,' she said quietly, turning to face him. Her expression was softer but there were still barriers between them that she was not prepared to lower.

'I'll be leaving soon. Can we not part as friends?'

'Friends?' She repeated the word in a wondering voice as though she did not understand fully what it meant.

'Yes. We could ride together. You could show me where you like to ride best, and I could tell you about my home on the other side of the mountains.' He watched her face closely when he asked her to show him where she liked to ride, and indeed, a flicker of wariness seemed to pass across it. But in the end she nodded, leading the way to the two horses. There were no saddles or bridles but she leapt on to the white mare's back and trotted off holding her silver mane, looking back with a challenge in her eyes to where Neil stood beside Flame irresolute, wondering if he would be able to ride Flame without a saddle and bridle and whether she would take him back to the Devil Stones. But she was already leaving him behind and so he stopped wondering, and followed her.

She had not taken the road he expected, and it was clear she was not going to repeat her ride of the night before. She turned her shoulder to the moors and took the coastal path, past the square stone church. In front of it there was a close knot of people, most of the village in fact – one man talking and gesticulating, the others listening and nodding and looking grave. For a moment Neil fancied he saw a dark haze enclosing them as though they were plotting something evil and the darkness of their hearts was projecting outwards to form an almost tangible miasma around them, and then he shook his head and blinked away the image. When he looked again he could not see it and chided himself for an over-active imagination, resenting the fact that the strange atmosphere of the place was apparently beginning to affect his reason.

Mairi had ridden on with scarcely a glance at the crowd and was already far ahead. Neil encouraged Flame to hurry and soon caught her up on the path that skirted the sea's inlet, high above the little harbour.

'What is going on at the Church?' he asked her as he drew level.

She shook her head and shrugged and rode on ahead with a sudden spurt of speed.

'She knows,' he thought. 'She knows.' And there was an icy feeling of foreboding in his heart.

The day was pleasant and the sun was warm. Neil soon pushed aside the memory of what he had seen and concentrated on keeping up with Mairi. Her black hair flowed out behind her and her legs, bare and brown, gripped the flanks of her mare strongly and confidently. There was none of the sullen shyness about her now that he had noticed before.

On the summit of the third hill Mairi put out her hand to touch Flame's neck, indicating that they should stop. Then, with a little smile, she gestured at the scene that lay before them. He sensed that what she was showing him was very special to her and she was expecting him to be impressed. Below them on the seaward side of the hill there was a broad arc of pure white sand stretching right around a bay, the water so azure and clear it seemed that they could see the very roots of the islands beneath its surface. And then, having paused long enough to be sure that he had seen and appreciated the place, she whispered to Moon-Metal and started the descent towards the beach. Slowly, stepping carefully at first, Flame and his master followed.

When they reached the cool clear water of a little stream that was threading towards the sea from the moors, the two animals stopped. Both riders dismounted and, cupping the fresh water in their hands, drank thirstily.

'This is almost as good a beach as the ones we have at Uig,' Neil said, wiping his mouth on the back of his hand.

'Almost?' she said indignantly.

'Almost,' he insisted.

She laughed and was up on Moon-Metal's back before he could blink.

'There is no beach as beautiful as this!' she cried, and she and the white mare were off again, wading through the river-reeds and out onto the flat to gallop over the sand, crackling the long thin razor shells and the Tyrian purple molluscs under her hooves.

He followed, feeling the salt wind from the sea sting his cheeks, seeing the water sparkling as the sun caught the breakers, hearing the shrill call of the gannets.

'Mairi!' he called for the joy of hearing her name. 'Mairi!'

He knew that the sound would be blown backwards and would never reach her. Moon-Metal . . . white horse on a white beach, caught in spindrift and sunlight! Flame could not catch her!

After a while Neil gave up trying and slowed his pace to a walk, sitting comfortably, enjoying the birds flying and the water rippling.

When she reached the end of the beach where the cliffs came down sharply to the sea, she turned and walked back. He could see her in the distance, like a black feather on a white bird. He was reminded of how she had looked among the Devil's Stones – enclosed in a private world – strong and happy.

He slid from Flame's back and stayed where he was, musingly throwing flat pebbles onto the water, watching them flip and spark as they touched and skimmed, watching the gannets dive and reap the sea of its crop of fishes time and again.

When she returned to him her cheeks were glowing and her eyes were shining. There were no shadows between them now and he knew that he had been accepted as her friend, perhaps the only one she had ever known apart from the silver-white mare.

They walked the beach together. Not many words passed between them – but many thoughts.

It was only when they left the beach to return to the village, walking the horses, that he described Uig to her. He spoke of his family briefly – but mostly he spoke about Brother Durston, his great friend, the Christian hermit. He described him as a strange, ungainly man, living like an animal in a byre yet more learned than the great earls of the Mainland – a man who had travelled the world and talked with princes and kings, and yet who had chosen to live in a simple hut of stone and turf high above the ocean on the headland near his father's farm.

Neil told her he could not understand the man. 'To have had so much travel and adventure – to be able to go anywhere in the world – to be so learned he could do anything – be the equal or the superior of anyone – and yet to give it all up and be content to live alone – with nothing!'

She listened intently and it was clear that she understood better than Neil the choice the hermit had made.

'He is not alone,' she said. 'He has more than the great earls, more than the kings and princes.'

'Don't you get restless?' Neil asked her. 'Don't you long to get away from here, to see the rest of the world, to meet new people, to wear fine clothes and jewels and eat delicious meals?'

She smiled and shook her head.

He thought about the drudgery of her life. How could she be content with it? He thought of the Tall Stones. Would she be as content if she could not ride to them in the secret hours of the night?

As though she wanted to be spared more questions, she took Moon-Metal into a trot and drew away from him. For the rest of the way they did not speak.

* * * *

The harbour was deserted as they rode by – boats drawn up at low tide – not a sign of anyone mending nets or preparing the boats for the next catch. There was no one walking on the quay side – no one sitting by the lobster pots. Without consciously noticing how unusual this was, they began to feel uneasy.

When they breasted the hill that overlooked the rest of the village they could see at once that a crowd had gathered outside Mairi's house.

As though Flame and Moon-Metal had read their thoughts, they came to an instant halt.

'What is it?' Neil whispered, frowning. The girl said nothing, but Neil could see that she knew. All the light had gone out of her face.

'Wait here,' he said. 'I'll go down and see what the matter is.'

But she followed him.

Once nearer, they could see the mob of people were shouting at the closed door of Mairi's house, banging their fists upon it, screaming curses, throwing stones. Her parents had barred it from the inside and were probably crouching terrified in the darkness. People were even trying to get in at the byre door, but this too had been barred.

'For the love of Jesus!' exclaimed Neil. 'What is going on?' He looked at Mairi and she was ashen – white and trembling, like a ghost on her ghost-white mane.

Suddenly he knew – and decided that he must get her away, fast. But someone had seen them.

'There she is!' was the shout, and the whole menacing crowd turned from the house and advanced on them. They were near enough now for him to recognize faces, yet their faces were almost unrecognizable – their eyes glazed with hate – their mouths twisted with the ugly words they were shouting. It seemed they had ceased to be individuals and become one composite being – welded together by a single dark force. Most of the village was there, but there were also some unknown faces. People had evidently come from other villages to join in the sport.

The children who had been standing back from the rest watching rather than joining in, ran excitedly towards them now, parroting the words they heard their elders use. 'Devil' and 'witch' they screamed, their high and piping voices adding a shrill counterpoint to the deep and angry rumble of the men's voices. One thick-set man, a stranger to the village, stooped and picked up a stone and suddenly everyone was following suit.

The door of the house burst open and Mairi's mother rushed out screaming. Thinly her voice carried to them, telling them to 'Go! Go! Go!'

Neil was already turning Flame around and pulling with his other hand on the mane of Mairi's mare, when the first rock was thrown. It missed her but she was so shocked she might have stayed rooted to the spot, unable to grasp what was happening to her had Neil not acted so promptly. With his help she stayed on Moon-Metal's back and with his help she galloped away. Moon-Metal and Flame . . . Quicksilver and Fire . . . fleeing from a blind and dangerous beast . . .

Neil and Mairi did not know where they were going, they knew only that they must go far, and behind them the day that had been so bright and beautiful was lying dead.

When the horses had run themselves out, and Neil could feel their weariness, he allowed them to stop. Gently he lifted Mairi down and she sank wearily onto a rock. He rubbed the horses with handfuls of heather and grass, talking to them quietly to calm them, knowing that they too had been afraid.

There are not many things more fearful than what is familiar and ordinary becoming suddenly alien and hostile. When he had finished he brought Mairi water from the stream cupped in his hands. She drank from them gratefully and then put her whole face in his cool, wet hands. He could feel her skin hot from weeping and brought more water for her to bathe her face. He did not need to ask why the villagers had turned against her and called her 'witch'. He remembered the other dark figure he had seen spying on her at the Devil's Stones.

'Tell me,' he asked hesitatingly, 'do you often visit those . . . those . . . that place?'

She did not reply, but lowered her head onto her knees and sat bowed, her whole body expressing such hopelessness, such loneliness, that he wished he had not asked the question and determined to ask no more. It was clear that the villagers were convinced that she was trafficking with the devil by visiting the tall stones. It was equally clear to him now, though it had not been the night before, that she was not. He was convinced that whatever she had done she was innocent of any evil intent. His face darkened with anger when he thought of the scene they had just witnessed. 'If anyone is trafficking with the devil . . .' he thought bitterly, remembering the change in the faces he had seen.

But after anger came sober consideration. What were they to do? It was summer and there would not be much darkness in the night, but there would be cold. Neither had a jacket. They were tired and they were hungry. The wind was already stronger and colder than it had been.

'I must go home,' she said suddenly. 'I must see if my mother is all right.'

'You cannot go back to your house,' he said sharply.

'I must.'

'You cannot,' he repeated. 'We'll find a sheltered and hidden place for you and Moon-Metal, and then I will go back alone.'

She was too exhausted to argue and dumbly followed him as he led the horses to a gully out of the wind's reach. He pulled up heather and grass and little soft plants until he had enough to make a small warm nest for her. There were no trees with branches to roof it, the Vikings had seen to that, but the old heather bushes were sometimes large enough to make a tolerable covering for her.

'You will be safe here for a while. You are well hidden,' Neil said, looking down at her. She did not reply, but he could see by the way she looked at him that she was grateful.

'I'll be as quick as I can,' he promised. 'You mustn't be anxious.'

She said nothing.

He stood staring down at her. Why did she creep off in the

dead of night to visit the Devil's Stones? Could there be some truth in the mob's accusations?

As though she picked up his thought her face darkened and she turned her back on him, nestling into the heather wall.

It was almost as though she had become part of the earth. Her dark hair flowed into the shadows. Broken twigs of heather clung to her clothes.

He stood for a long time – hesitating – unwilling to leave her. But at last he turned away.

'I'll be back,' he said quietly. 'As soon as I'm sure your mother is safe.'

She lay unmoving. The ancient earth had folded her in its arms. She was its child.

Chapter 4

The Dream

The village was quiet – the one muddy street deserted – when Neil finally arrived. He walked Flame quietly to the long low cottage of Mairi's parents.

Not knowing what the situation would now be, he decided he would try to attract Mairi's mother's attention without alerting her father to his presence. He was sure Braden's sympathies would be more with the mob than with his daughter.

He remembered a tune he had whistled the evening before. It was a tune handed down from the days of the Viking raids: a signal the islanders used as a warning or to let captured Islanders know that help was near. Now that the days of fear and fire were supposedly over, the Islanders, many of them with Viking blood flowing in the same veins as Island blood, whistled the tune only for pleasure. He had been whistling it when he had been rubbing down his horse the evening before. Mairi's mother had smiled at him as though she had recognised it. He hoped now that she would recognise it again.

He started the tune softly, standing beside the doorway, stroking Flame's neck to keep him quiet, constantly looking around to make sure that no one else would hear. On the third repetition there was a sound from inside the cottage and Neil tensed, clenching his fists in case it were Braden. He heard the wooden bolt drawn back cautiously and the rickety door pulled open a crack. He could not see the eye that must have been looking out at him, but he knew that it was there. He repeated the tune, but it was now no more than a breath, all sound had gone from it, and in his heart was the fear that must have been there whenever the tune was used in the old days.

The door opened further and he was relieved to see that Mairi's mother was alone. Her face was red and blotched with weeping.

'Is your husband . . .?' he whispered.

She shook her head. But she was frightened.

'She must not come here,' she breathed. 'You must keep her away.'

'She is safe. Don't worry. I have come back only because she was anxious about you.'

The woman began weeping again, shaking her head and trying to push him away.

'I must talk to you,' he said urgently.

'No . . . no . . . you must go!' she sobbed.

'I must talk to you,' he repeated and took her arm and pushed her back into the house. Still holding Flame, he guided him through the narrow low door. Once inside he led him through the room to the cattle stall at the far end and then returned to the hearth where the woman was distractedly poking at the almost exhausted peat fire, trying to get some extra heat for the black cauldron she had hanging from a long iron chain above it. There would be mutton broth in there, Neil thought, and he was hungry.

'I must have food and warm clothes for her,' he said. 'But first I must know why it is that the people in this village hate her so much. What has she done?'

Blindly the woman stirred the pot. Delicious hot smells rose from it. Neil swallowed, his eyes smarting from the smoke that had risen at she disturbed the smouldering peat.

She made no move to answer, her face as closed as Mairi's had been. He strode up to her and removed the long ladle from her hand, roughly pushing her back from the fire.

'Listen to me. Answer me. If I am to help her I must know!'

'They . . . they think she is a witch,' the woman sobbed.

'Do *you* think she is a witch?' Neil asked sharply.

'I . . . I don't know . . .'

'Your own daughter?'

'It's ever since the horse . . .'

'You never told me who gave it to her.'

'The Devil.'

'Now you know that is not true,' Neil said surprised at the confidence with which he said this.

'Who gave it to her? Tell me.' He put down the ladle and took the woman by both arms and shook her. She did not answer, but hung her head. She was terrified. Of what? The fierceness of the way he was confronting her, or of something she knew – too terrible to tell.

'Tell me!'

'She . . . she found it . . .'

'Found it? Where?'

'Among the Devil Stones. She *would* go there. I told her not to – but she would go.'

'She just found it among those Stones!' Neil could feel every individual hair prickling on his scalp and a strange cold feeling in his limbs. He knew that he was committed to helping the girl. He knew that he could not abandon her now when she had no one, but – he began for the first time to realize that he might be meddling with something he could not handle. He had had experience of fighting and had outwitted many enemies already in his life. At home in Uig there was only one of his brothers who could equal him in strength. But the Devil and his dark hordes . . . He crossed himself and whispered a fervent prayer for protection. He wished Brother Durston, the hermit who lived at Uig, was here. This kind of fighting was more in his line.

'It is a Saracen breed,' he found himself saying, 'from the Mainland. King William brought such horses from Normandy. My own Flame is such a one.' Even as he said it he remembered that Saracens were supposed to be in league with the Devil. Had not the Christian English since King William's day gone on Crusades to wrest the Holy Places from them?

The woman had stopped crying and was looking at him for the first time straight in the eye.

'Why was it among those Stones?' she asked. 'Why has no one sought it? Why has no one claimed it?'

Neil was silent. He had let her arms drop and she had taken

up the ladle again, scooping him out some broth into a wooden bowl. He drank it thankfully, his senses taking in the taste, the smell, the heat, while his thoughts tried out a dozen explanations for the presence of the mare among the Stones.

'If it is the Devil's steed – why is it so gentle and good natured?' he asked.

Skena shrugged. 'The Devil knows how to play tricks.'

Neil frowned.

'I don't believe it is the Devil's gift,' he said firmly.

'But it is not only the mare,' she said. 'There have been . . . other things.'

'What things?'

'Signs.'

'What signs?'

'Just before you came the people were questioning Mairi about things she had said and things she had done . . . She was accused of being a witch and she denied it. Just at that moment a star fell out of the sky.'

'I saw it!' cried Neil. 'I saw it with my own eyes.'

'You see!' said the mother, shrugging hopelessly.

'But that does not mean . . .'

'It was a sign from God that she was lying . . .'

'It may have been a sign from God that she was telling the truth!'

Skena shook her head sadly. She had tried to tell them that, but they had shouted her down, telling her that it was the proof of the devil's mark on Mairi because Lucifer had fallen from heaven just as that star had fallen.

Neil was silent for a while, thinking. He could not, would not believe that the girl who had raced her silver mare along the seas edge, joy and the love of living blowing back from her like streamers of light, could possibly be in the clutches of the Evil One. 'By their works shall ye know them' the Gospel said . . . Surely the shouting of curses and the stoning of a living creature was more the work of the Devil than anything she had done?

'Do you think your daughter is a witch?' he asked, looking deeply and seriously into her eyes.

'My husband says . . .'

'No. I am not asking you what your husband says. I am asking you what *you* think. You gave birth to the girl. You have looked after her every moment of her life. What do *you* think?'

There was a long pause. Neil did not take his eyes off hers. He could see the conflict that was going on between her mother's love and the thoughts that had been put into her mind by her husband and her neighbours.

'I . . . think . . .' she said at last, the words coming from her with great difficulty, wrung from the depths of the heart which had been untouched by the harsh suspicions and prejudices of the society she lived in. 'I think that she is not a witch. She has gifts that God has given her and because . . . because we do not have them . . . we fear her . . .'

Neil could have hugged the woman.

'Mother, you have spoken true. I know it. I feel it in my heart. And now you must tell me more about these gifts . . . and we must think together how to help her.'

For the first time since he had first seen her the woman looked happy and strong. He felt he had reached the real person behind the shadowy mask. She started to speak but a sound outside startled both of them and she fell silent, fear returning.

'You must go,' she whispered nervously. 'The only way to help her is to take her away from here. Take her far away. Let no one from this village know where she is. Let her start again among people who do not fear her . . .'

'Her father . . .?'

'Her father will beat her if she returns, and turn her over to the villagers. He has beaten her before . . .' The woman's face was dark again with the pain of the memory of standing helplessly by as her man thrashed the young girl. He had called it 'trying to drive the devil out'.

Neil thought quickly. Her mother was right. He would take her away and bring her back only when the villagers had calmed down and he could prove her innocence. Now he must go and he must not lead them back to her.

He looked around. The farmer would soon be coming through

the door. He saw Flame's saddle and beside it the light one that Mairi used for Moon-Metal. He rushed to the door of the byre and pulled at the table that had been placed against it to strengthen it when the angry crowd were trying to break their way in. Skena was gathering up warm clothes and food and thrust a bundle into his hand just as he got the door clear. Seizing the saddles and the bundle he whistled to Flame and together they crept out as the other door opened and Mairi's father came striding in.

When he reached the small gully where he had left Mairi he found that she was no longer there. Shadows were deep as the brief northern night held the Island fast. He thought perhaps that he had come to the wrong place and rode up to the top of the hill again to survey the surroundings. But every landmark he had memorized was in its place. He picked his way back to the gully and called to her and whistled for Moon-Metal, thinking perhaps that she was hiding against the approach of a stranger. But the whole landscape was silent and he could feel that there was no living creature near apart from the tiny insects that lived in the earth and under the cover of the heather, and even they had suspended their tiny creakings and rustlings as though waiting fearfully for him to leave.

He slipped from Flame's back and sat wearily down burying his head on his knees. What should he do? One part of his mind told him to return home to Uig and forget the girl. Her problems were not his problems. He had come to buy a mare. The mare was not for sale. There was no more to it. But the other part of his mind, the deeper part, knew that he could not leave her. He thought about her, lonely and afraid, fleeing from her home and everything and everyone that she had ever known. What would she do? Where could she go? She had nothing with her; no family names she would dare to use to help her claim a hearth in a new village. She would be a stranger always, a wanderer accompanied everywhere by the fear of violation and sudden death at the hands of other strangers, other wanderers. Without a family and a hearth the world would be a vast and hollow place. Travelling was his greatest pleasure, but he always knew that the hearth of his home was there waiting for him when he was tired, and the eyes of his family would light up to see him at his return no matter how long he had been away. Their arms would enfold him. A bed would be prepared.

Flame and he were exhausted. Wearily he lay down in the hollow nest she had left – trying not to think.

'When I am rested . . .' he told himself. 'When I have slept . . .'

He drifted off to sleep almost immediately.

And then it seemed to him that he had become part of the mist that formed with the night, winding like a ghost among other ghosts through the valleys and over the meres, drawn by some unseen force to lie at the foot of Callanish hill. And there – without limbs to move or tongue to call – he saw her walking the long avenue in the pale light just before dawn, the Stones clear of the mist, shining and powerful. Her back was straight – her eyes clear. She was clad in a long cloak that flowed like silver water behind her. Stars gleamed from her midnight hair.

With her were others, men and women, young children, babes in arms . . . all following a tall figure in a long and flowing cloak of feathers, wearing a crown of eagle feathers on his head. In the air above him, circling like a second crown, that formed and reformed every moment, was a cloud of tiny birds, of wrens . . .

Neil was filled with a longing to join the procession, a feeling that among these people there was joy on the deepest level, the joy of being in step with a great and noble purpose . . . Briefly he felt that he was drifting from the valley up the hill and then a shadow crossed his thinking and in it he found doubt and taboo. What God was this these alien people worshipped? Surely it could not be the same that the Gospels taught. He floated back to the valley and after that no matter how hard he tried to move independently of the general mist he could not. He saw the feathered Priest lift his arms to the rising sun, but that was the last thing he saw as the mist swirled away.

When he was conscious again he found himself back in the

nest of heather he had prepared for Mairi, the sharp stems prick-
ing his skin. 'Why not . . .?' he found himself murmuring as he
woke. 'Why not the same God . . . always . . . from before the
Beginning . . . to beyond the End . . . the same God – but with
different names – clothed in different forms – not because the
great He/She is different – but because there is no way we can
visualize the true form of the ultimate Divinity, and we have to
use only what images are familiar to us.'

The chill, crystal clear light of dawn was banishing shadow.

He shook himself and stood up. Climbing out of the sheltering gully he stood on the hill top shivering in the breeze, looking
out over the softly shining water that lay everywhere between
the islands of Loch Roag. Could she have gone back to the
Stones of Callanish? He did not notice that he no longer thought
of them as the Devil's Stones. He tried to tell himself that what
he had experienced so vividly was only a dream, but it was not
fading as a dream should. It was still in his mind as clearly as
the memory of the previous day.

A bird winged overhead giving a loud glad cry that the day
had arrived. He must make a decision. He remembered how
happy and peaceful she had been when he had first seen her
among the tall Stones. Although it would be foolish to go there
now given the suspicions of the villagers, she might well have
done so, clinging to the feelings of security and peace that she
had found there in the past and which she now could find nowhere else.

Yes, he would look there before anywhere else.

To reach the headland he had to skirt widely round Kirkoway.
The ride was long and the sun already climbing steadily. He
touched Flame to a gallop.

He passed no one on the track and was glad of it. His only
witnesses were some sheep on a hillside and a wild pony that
looked up from grazing when it heard Flame's hooves hammering the peat. When he came in sight of the Stones he thought
back to his first impression of them and smiled ruefully. Who
was he to criticise the villagers for superstition when he himself had been in such terror?

Now in the sunlight the place was beautiful and bright. He reined Flame in and rode slowly and quietly up the slope of the hill, confident that she would be there, careful not to startle her.

At first he did not see her. It was the whinny of Moon-Metal greeting Flame that gave her away. She was crouching at the foot of the tallest stone, her head against it and her arms around it, frail and tired. She did not greet him when he approached her but turned her face to the stone as a small child might turn its face to the shoulder of its mother when uneasy about the approach of a stranger.

He still sat upon Flame's back and he towered above her. She was not as he had seen her in his dream. Her homespun tunic was muddy, her hair windblown and matted, her shoulders thin and hunched. The hand that clutched the rough stone was scratched and bleeding.

'Mairi,' he said softly. She did not look up.

He dismounted and Flame moved away to join Moon-Metal. The two stood quietly cropping as Neil stood beside the girl in the inner circle. He longed to reach out to touch her but hesitated to do so.

The place was very quiet. The breeze that had chilled him at dawn had a little more body to it now, but it made no sound as it stirred among the heather and the grasses. Neil had the feeling that it was in fact making a sound but that he could no longer hear it. He frowned slightly. There was a touch of magic about the place after all. He reached out his hand towards the girl several times but found that he had to draw it back. Whether it was his awe of the place and the memory of her as he had seen her in his dream, or whether there was indeed a Presence there preventing him touching her he could not decide.

'Mairi,' he repeated.

This time she turned her head and looked up at him. Her eyes were deeply hurt and afraid.

He squatted down beside her. 'This is no place to be,' he said gently. 'They'll surely look for you here.'

'It is home,' she whispered in a voice so low that he had to bend nearer to catch the words. 'It is where I belong.'

'You must not say that,' he said, trying to sound firm and authoritative. 'No one belongs here but the wind and . . . ghosts,' he added.

'No ghosts,' she said. 'My people. My friends.'

'What people? What friends?'

'I saw them last night. I have seen them before.'

'Who are they?'

'They are the people who came here in ancient times.' She pointed to the silver water of the Loch. 'They came over the sea in ships and built this temple.'

'Temple?' In spite of his vision of the night before, in spite of the thoughts that had come to him on waking, he still trembled at the word 'temple' and associated it with pagan gods, pagan demons.

She had stopped clinging to the rock now and was looking at him directly, eager for him to understand.

'My friend, the High Priest, is good. There is no evil in him. He talks of a Great Spirit who created all things and he wears a cloak of feathers to show that his spirit can fly like the birds to reach up to the Great Spirit. Real birds fly around his head unafraid, showing him the way . . .'

Neil jumped up, his skin prickling.

She stood up too, her face suddenly full of light.

'You have seen them too! You have seen them!'

'No,' he said sharply. 'No, I have not.'

'I saw recognition in your eyes.'

'It was only something in a dream. I had a dream last night.'

'In dreams sometimes . . . my people have told me . . . when the surface of the mind is asleep it is possible to see into the great depths where all things are . . .'

'It was just a dream.'

'Some dreams are different from other dreams. Could you not feel that it was different?'

'How different?'

'Most dreams are full of things from the day . . . worries and fears and memories . . . bits and pieces that float about for a while and then disappear. But some dreams are very strong.

They are given to us to show us something special. They teach us something that we need to know. And when we wake they do not go away, but stay in the memory with every detail clear.'

Neil was silent. He could remember every detail of his dream.

'Holy Scripture tells us of such dreams,' she said. 'And there are Seers and prophets who are called on to interpret them.'

'Holy Scripture also warns us against witches and false prophets who try to lead us away from truth.' As he said this he wished that he had not, for the eager, trusting light went out of her face, her shoulders slumped and she turned her face back to the Stone.

Impulsively he stepped forward and put his hands on her shoulders. She tried to shrug them away, but he held firm. He tried to turn her to him, but she resisted.

'Mairi,' he said. 'I am sorry. I did not mean . . . Mairi, I am your friend. Trust me. All this is so new to me. I don't know what to believe any more. I want to help you. Don't turn from me like that.' But she continued to pull away from him. 'Look at me. Feel me. I am flesh and blood. Not a dream.' He put his hands on the side of her face and forced her to turn her head. She shut her eyes. Tears were seeping out from under her lids and creeping down her pale cheeks.

He looked at her silently for a few moments and then lent forward and kissed her gently on the forehead. He felt her tremble as he did so. The tension in her body relaxed slightly, and she no longer pulled so fiercely away from him. He touched her cheek with his lips. Her mouth was very close. He hesitated, feeling his own body tremble, realizing that her closeness felt very different to him suddenly.

She opened her eyes and looked into his.

It seemed a long time that they were so poised, looking into each other's eyes, afraid to take the further step. It seemed to him that he could hear his own heart beating at the centre of a great silence and stillness. It seemed to him that he could not have moved even if he had wanted to. His thoughts seemed to hover round the edges of his mind in such a way that he was aware that they were there, but that he could not tell what they were.

Suddenly Flame, who had wandered over to a rich patch of grass near them, snorted. Neil sprang up, startled, reaching instinctively for the knife at his belt. But there was no knife there. Then, seeing that it was Flame, he looked at Mairi embarrassed. She laughed as she held out the knife he had left with her for protection in her nest of heather. He grinned as he took it from her.

'It is this place,' he said. 'It makes me nervous.'

She stood up, looking calmer, and went over to Flame and stroked his head. He nuzzled against her affectionately. Neil watched, thinking that he had heard that animals could always sense evil and the supernatural. 'Beware of someone animals fear and hate,' his mother had told him. He was ashamed that he had moments of doubt about the girl. She was no witch, no handmaid of the devil. Of that he was now sure.

He looked at Moon-Metal curiously, remembering what Skena had told him. How had this fine mare come to be wandering unattended in such a place? It was obvious she was no wild creature, but had been tended and trained lovingly. The mystery of it reminded him that whatever he thought about Mairi, the villagers still thought she was to be feared and had been ready to stone her to death just a few hours before. Whether they had thought better of it by now or not, he was not prepared to risk her returning to her family. He resolved to take her to his own home.

He turned round and found that she had left Flame's side and was standing in front of the tallest Stone, the one she had previously been clinging to. She was standing far enough back from it so that she could look up to the top of it and was staring at something with great intensity. Neil followed the direction of her eyes curiously, half expecting to see some ghoulish face. What he did see startled him almost as much. He had looked at that flat white crystal face before, but had not noticed that in the centre near the top, like the eye of a cyclops, was a single large black crystal.

She was staring into this with all her attention and a very strange expression.

'Mairi!' he said sharply. But she seemed not to hear.

'Mairi!' he called again, this time hurrying to her side and seizing her arm. 'What are you doing? What are you thinking? We must go from this place *at once*.' He pulled her quite roughly from the ridge of earth and heather that had given her the height to outstare the uncanny black eye.

She looked bewildered, stumbling against him and almost falling.

'No, Neil, no . . .' she almost sobbed. 'Let me stay. This is my place. This is where I have to be.'

'Nonsense,' he said brusquely, and gave her a tug towards the horses.

'You go,' she said, pulling away from him. 'These are my people. I belong here.' He knew that she did not mean her family and her village but the ancient people of the Stones long since dead.

'You are coming away from here!' he said fiercely and picked her up in his arms. She struggled to free herself. 'We are going to my home and there we will talk about whether these people are your people or not. If when we are away from this place . . . far away . . . you can convince me that this is where you ought to be, I'll bring you back. I promise,' he added hastily as he caught her expression. At this she stopped struggling. Whether she believed he would bring her back or whether she at last realised that he was too strong for her and she could not break his grip, he could not tell. He lifted her onto Flame's back and climbed up behind her. Tears were streaming down her face as she looked back over his shoulder.

As they galloped away, the tall Stones of Callanish stood impassively against the sky, guarding the ancient sacred place, staring with their one dark eye at the waters of the loch, the islands beyond, and far over the unfathomable great ocean that stretched beyond man's comprehension into the regions known only in myth and legend and possibly to the ancient people who had first built this strange and potent temple.

Moon-Metal followed close behind, tossing her silver mane.

Chapter 5

The House of Power

It was only when they were well out of sight and reach of the Callanish Stones that Neil permitted Mairi to ride the white mare. She seemed to be resigned to following his lead and made no attempt to turn back. How different everything looked now from the way it had looked the first time he rode beside these glassy meres. It seemed as though a long time had passed and he looked back at himself then as though he had been a child. He had the same face, the same limbs – but his thoughts were not the thoughts of the same person.

When the sunlight was snuffed out by clouds and the air chilled, Mairi wrapped herself in the shawl Skena had sent with him. He rode up close to her and reached out his hand to help her tuck the shawl in firmly against the wind. His fingers touched her cheek and her shoulder and trembled as they lingered on her waist.

Black clouds were rolling up over the crags above Glen Valtos when they reached it. Beyond these mountains lay the comfortable green hills and the silver sands of his home, and the only way to reach them was through this narrow gorge. Neil knew it would be more sensible to take shelter and wait the storm out on this side of the chasm – but he sensed that beneath the fragile shell of Mairi's silence lay turmoil. He wanted to get her home. He wanted to set her by the hearth and for her to know that she had a place among the living that she could call 'home', and people among the living that she could call her 'people'. He chose to hurry forward.

Mairi looked around her fearfully as they took the narrow

path between towering cliffs of rock. The clouds pressed down, shutting out the sky. They seemed to be entering a dark and sinister passage through which the wind howled and moaned, trying to push them back. But Neil would not be pushed.

'Hurry!' he shouted against the wind. 'We'll be safe on the other side of this.'

Safe? Mairi felt the huge storm was hovering over them just as a kestrel hovers over a field mouse. She knew now what the field mouse must feel as the kestrel's wings cut out the sun-light.

Neil started to gallop, the white mare following. The two beasts tossed their manes. They could feel it too – the fear. Mairi bound her shawl as close as she could about her, her cheeks stinging with the cold of the wind, her eyes watering.

'Faster!' Neil's voice was powerful and strange, his words echoing against the cliffs. The danger was a challenge. He was excited. He was breaking free! He was outwitting the dark forces! Mairi could see his teeth bared in a grin as he looked over his shoulder at her. But she could not smile back at him. She was leaving all that she had known to ride through this dark place with him. And on the other side – would she ever see her people again?

A few heavy drops of rain drove into her face.

'Faster!' yelled Neil, knowing now that he had made a mis-take, but they had gone too far into the gorge to turn back.

And then the storm broke! The white mare screamed as light-ning split the sky and thunder cracked immediately – like a giant whip. The rain drove into their faces with such force that it became impossible to go on.

Neil seized the mare's bridle and dragged both horses under the shelter of an overhang. Mairi slid exhausted into his arms and he lowered her to a rocky ledge. There they crouched against the cliff face as the storm roared and raged. The Glen was like a funnel down which the ancient storm gods rode their battle charge. Moon-Metal and Flame shied at every thunder-clap, staring with wide and terrified eyes at the fury around them – tugging at the bridles that had been fastened to the rock. Neil stroked and cajoled the animals – trying to imbue in them a confidence he himself did not feel. Mairi leaned against his chest, held firm by his left arm. Together they tried to calm their steeds – and to a certain extent they succeeded. Neil put his lips to Mairi's cheek and drank the icy water that was running down her face. He held her closer . . . closer . . . It seemed to him there was no past or future – no earth or sky beyond where they were – no feeling like the feeling that was coursing through his veins. She was part of him. Part of the rock and the water and the lightning and the thunder. Even the horses were part of this feeling – their muscular flanks pressing against them – driving them back against the rock cliff . . .

Then suddenly Neil became aware that another sound had joined the cacophony and this one brought a frown to his face.

Every rock was running with water and huge waterfalls had appeared, gushing white from the tops of the cliffs. The hard, impervious gneiss soaked up nothing. The river was swelling every moment and he could hear it rolling boulders over further up the glen. It was already well over the track and washing over their feet.

He looked up the sheer cliffs and cursed himself for being such a fool. He should have known he could not beat the storm. Why had he tried? Why? Why?

But it was no good wasting time on regrets now. They must get out of this trap, and fast!

He noticed a slope to the left that, though steep, was not insurmountable. Without a word he led Flame out into the full blast of the downpour and then, slipping and sliding, started to climb. Mairi struggled to follow him, dodging the small rocks and pebbles that he dislodged. They reached a safe ledge at last and watched with horror as the swirling and angry brown waters of the swollen river came hurtling down the valley, sweeping fiercely over the very place that they had been so shortly before, obliterating all signs of the path on which they had travelled.

* * * *

They were forced to spend the night on the ledge, huddled together, wet and shivering. Eventually the rain ceased but the water still rushed into the valley from the waterfalls on the cliffs – and the brown and turbulent flood showed no sign of abating. The clouds cleared at last and the moon shone out, filling the noisy glen with a combination of deep shadow and glinting light. Neil stared at its eerie beauty and listened to the powerful water sounds. He remembered that the word 'valtos' meant 'house of power' in the language of the Vikings. He had never understood it until now. House of Power! Mighty house of the powerful thunder god of the Norsemen!

Mairi had fallen exhausted against his shoulder and was sleeping. He looked down at her, wonderingly, her dark lashes lying against her cheek as gently and innocently as feathers. They had narrowly escaped death. Had her unholy magic unleashed this storm upon their heads and stirred his own body to such a frenzy that he endangered their lives? With his free hand he quietly made the sign of the cross over her and then, just in case, a rune sign to placate the Norse gods of the glen.

By mid-morning they were able to move again and, weak from their ordeal, half scrambled, half fell down the slippery steep slope to the rock-strewn track. Mairi looked ill and was coughing and shaking, her eyes unnaturally bright. Neil took her on his own horse so that he could keep her from falling, and Moon-Metal stepped daintily behind. There was no question of galloping now. The ground was treacherous and their progress was slow.

The water sounds of the chasm through which they picked their way had changed. The rough harsh roaring of the night had given way to strong melodious music as the water in the valley flowed over and around the various boulders in its path. From the sheer rock walls the waterfalls still fell, but they were now only thin lines of silver, each with its own sound shaped by the rock over which it passed: some glancing lightly from outcrop to outcrop – threading a zig-zag path down the cliff, singing a complicated tune as it did so; others leaping off the top and falling unhindered to the river, the sun catching their drops as they fell and transmuting them to gold.

Neil began to worry what he was going to tell his family about Mairi. He could only tell them part of Mairi's story if he was to keep her safe. And all that he himself knew about her was only a small part of what there was to know.

The water bubbled and chattered and sang. A small bird leapt into the air from a twig that was clinging to the sheer rock wall, and darted, shrieking, past Flame's head. 'That bird will tell its own story to its mate,' Neil thought. 'And in that story we will be the terrible monsters it encountered in the glen. It will boast of how narrowly it escaped from our clutches. From its point of view the story is true, but from ours it is not.' Since the world began every story told has had many different versions – and who can say that there is only one truth?

His thoughts ran on and on, the water sounds mingling with them until he no longer distinguished them from his own thinking. Time passed until suddenly the cliffs fell away and the valley opened out. They climbed a hill and looked down on the wide, fine sand flats of Uig. Mairi gasped. She had thought her own beach was grand, but this was breathtaking. Hills like green hands spread the shining cloak of white sand almost as far as they could see. Far away the glint of water at its hem showed where the sea lay. Everything shone. Everything was pure. The air after the storm was so fresh each breath taken was as intoxicating as wine, as purifying as baptism.

'We are nearly home,' Neil said joyfully. Flame knew it too and started to canter and then to gallop. Moon-Metal whinnied and followed close behind.

Neil's farm was still an hour or so away and before they reached it they had to climb and descend several hills; but everything was now familiar to Neil and excitedly he pointed out place after place to his companion where this or that adventure had taken place. That was where the Vikings had landed in the old days, his own ancestors through his mother's line. There they had burnt a barn. There they had been defeated. There his father had met his mother. There his brother Donal had wrestled for the title of champion and had won three years running.

It was when he pointed to the last hill before his home that she asked if she could return to Moon-Metal and ride by herself. Neil reined in at once. He helped her down and as soon as her feet touched the earth Moon-Metal came up to her.

Neil noticed that she stumbled slightly as she moved to mount her mare and he wondered if he were doing right to let her ride alone. Her cheeks were bright red and her eyes feverish.

She managed to keep upright and Neil felt secretly proud of the two of them as they breasted the last hill and moved down the track to the great house that was his home. Her long black hair had dried out and flowed back over her shoulders gracefully. Moon-Metal almost danced.

There was the hill that overlooked the sea where Brother Durston's hermit cell weathered all storms. There was the long low house, the grandest in the district – for Neil's people were descended from a chief's second son. These were the horses that were Neil's special care, looking up from their cropping, sniffing the air, and then galloping towards them joyfully.

Fiona, his sister, and Ingrid, his mother, came to the door and stood waving as they made their triumphant arrival among the circling, skittish horses and the leaping, barking dogs. Even the geese clustered around, honking, and a cock stretched to its full height on a bundle of hay and crowed magnificently.

When they were at last in the muddy, much trampled forecourt, Neil leaped off Flame and ran to hug his mother and his sister. But Fiona's attention was only half on her brother. While she hugged him she was looking over his shoulder at the white mare that stood behind him. She scarcely noticed the young girl on its back. Her face shone, knowing that it was to be her wedding present. Already in her imagination she could see herself riding to meet her betrothed in her finest dress. After a very cursory hug she left Neil and rushed to the white horse.

'O, it is beautiful . . . beautiful!' she cried as she danced round it, and then her face clouded as she looked closer. 'But how it has been neglected! Look at its mane! It is all matted and muddy.'

She looked up at Mairi for the first time, seeing only a dark-haired peasant girl who should have kept her master's horse in better condition. For one brief moment Mairi's eyes met hers, blazing and hostile, and then the girl slipped forward and fell towards her in a dead faint. Neil turned in time to see her falling and rushed forward. He caught her just before she hit the ground.

Fiona was shocked.

'What on earth . . .?'

'She is ill,' Neil said quickly. 'We were caught in Glen Valtos in a storm and had to spend the night soaked to the skin and freezing. She is certainly feverish mother, can you do something for her?'

His mother hurried forward at once, full of pity for the girl, and fussed around her, feeling her burning forehead and her cheeks as Neil carried her to the house. Fiona stood back looking after her, remembering the anger in the girl's eyes.

'Why does she hate me?' she puzzled.

The three of them vanished into the house. Fiona turned to the white mare and looked at it thoughtfully.

'Shall I rub it down, Fee?' asked one of her younger brothers eagerly.

'No,' she said sharply. 'You look after Flame. This one is mine and no one else is going to touch her.'

Chapter 6

The Fever

Neil laid Mairi down on the bed and watched as his mother tended to her. Gradually the colour came back to her cheeks and her eyes opened. Neil leant forward eager to reassure her that she was among friends but her eyes, though open, did not look at him, nor indeed at anything in the room. She lifted her head with a great effort and stared beyond their heads at something or someone they could not see. Afraid that his mother might think what her own villagers had thought, Neil moved quickly and clumsily – staggering slightly as he took a step back knocking the earthenware bowl of water from the table with a crash. Ingrid at once began to bustle and scold.

'What's the matter with you?' she demanded. 'Are you ill too?' She put her cool hand to his forehead and shook her head. 'No fever – but you look pale.'

'I am tired mother,' he said. 'Nothing but tired.'

'Well, rest you must have then. Away with you and get some sleep. No, don't worry about her,' she added as she saw his anxious look. 'I will look after her.'

Mairi had fallen back again and lay curled under the sealskin rugs, her eyes closed, already well on the way to sleep.

'Bless her,' said Ingrid softly. 'Who is she?'

Neil took a deep breath. He had thought of several stories to tell his family, none of them completely the truth. He stood beside the bed now looking down at the girl. Her black hair was spread around her, her lashes very dark against her cheek. She looked frail, vulnerable and very beautiful.

'Her name is Mairi,' he said at last. 'The white mare is hers.

I could not persuade her to sell it to me so I brought her here hoping that she would change her mind when she met Fiona.'

His mother looked troubled. 'Fiona has thought of nothing else, spoken of nothing else but that mare since you left,' she said. 'She has set her heart on it. I hope we will not have to disappoint her.'

'I thought perhaps . . .' Neil said, and then paused.

'What?'

'That . . . that if Mairi still would not part with the white mare . . . I could give Fiona Flame instead. She has always coveted him and he is fit for any fine lady in any royal court.'

Ingrid looked surprised. She knew what a sacrifice that would be for him. He and Flame had been inseparable since the stallion's birth and she would not have thought he would have considered parting with him. She looked at the young girl on the bed thoughtfully. Was he in love with her? Had he brought her home as bride? She tightened her lips. She was not ready to part with Neil yet. It was bad enough that her daughter was leaving, but she was marrying a young man who would take her to live at Prince David's court in Scotia where she would have comforts and luxuries almost inconceivable to her hardworking mother. She knew that the girl had set her heart on riding out to meet him on her fine white mare and Ingrid believed that even if Neil meant what he said about parting with Flame – and she was by no means sure that he would not change his mind on the matter – Fiona would not accept the substitution. There was something very special about a pure white mare.

'We shall see,' said Neil's mother mildly, keeping her thoughts to herself. 'Now leave us. This poor child must sleep.'

Neil himself was hungry and exhausted. He left his mother the task of breaking the news about Moon-Metal to Fiona and retired in search first of food and then of sleep.

When he woke it was night and the house was silent. He lay for a while half asleep, enjoying the comfort of his bed after the rigours of the night before. He began to see pictures in his mind and he lay quietly watching them, making no judgements, thinking no thoughts: Mairi galloping along the white beach near her home joyous and happy . . . Mairi walking amongst strange people in a strange ritual . . . Mairi attacked and stoned . . . Mairi clinging to the tall Stone with the crystal eye at Callanish as though her life depended on it . . . In his half conscious state he saw no difference between the dream he had had of her walking in procession and his waking memories of her. It seemed perfectly acceptable to him that she was at once the young girl who lived in a peasant's cottage at Kirkoway, and the young woman he had seen with people who had apparently disappeared long, long before the Vikings . . .

'I must ask her what it was like to live in those days . . .' he thought drowsily, and then drifted off to sleep again.

In the morning when he was up and splashing cold water on his face, he found that it was more difficult to reconcile the two images of her.

Mairi was still feverish in the morning and Ingrid, worrying about her, suggested that Neil should ask Brother Durston's assistance.

Brother Durston was pleased to see Neil back from his expedition and listened with interest as he told him a quick and edited version of the story concerning Mairi. The tall, lean hermit with the penetrating dark eyes saw at once that he was only being told part of something that was genuinely worrying his young friend, but he asked no questions. As soon as he knew that his herbal skill was needed he stooped through the low door of his cell and disappeared into the interior.

The dry-stone hut was built against the hillside, the roof covered with turf. Inside, in a dim, bare space, there was a wooden bed covered with coarse homespun rugs, a few pots and pans near a central hearth and a small shelf on which Durston kept his precious gospel book, his chessmen and walrus-ivory carving tools, and his little leather pouches of dried herbs. These last he now rummaged amongst and, having found what he was looking for, stooped low again as he went through the door.

'Come, lad, we must see what we can do for your friend. From what you say rest and warmth is what she needs most . . . but we'll give her an elder-flower infusion for the fever and coltsfoot for her cough.'

The man's stride was long and even though Neil himself was tall he had almost to run to keep up with him.

'Brother Durston,' Neil started to say and then hesitated. The hermit did not look round at him but waited for him to feel easy enough in his mind to continue. Almost imperceptibly he slackened his pace so that the boy could more comfortably keep level with him. 'There may be more to her illness than just the chill she caught in the storm.'

'Oh?' said Brother Durston

Neil knew that he longed to tell Brother Durston the whole story, longed to share the burden of it, to ask his advice, but Brother Durston was a monk totally dedicated to the Christian religion. Would he too turn against Mairi and say that she was a pagan witch?

'She . . . she had some trouble at home before we left,' Neil ventured at last. 'Her father beat her and she ran away . . . I have not told my family yet. She . . . she has nowhere to go. I want to keep her here and look after her.'

'It is a serious matter taking such a young girl from her family, my son. Will they not send armed men to fetch her back?'

'Oh, no. I am sure they will not,' said Neil quickly, too quickly he realized afterwards. He hated lying to Brother Durston, but he still feared to tell him more of the story.

Brother Durston gave him a sideways glance, but before he could speak Fiona came storming out of the house like a sudden gust of wind.

'Oh no!' muttered Neil under his breath.

'What do you *mean*, she won't sell the mare? Why did you bring it here if you had no intention of letting me have it?' Fiona raged.

Brother Durston gave Neil a quizzical look, skirted round

her and disappeared into the house. Neil was left with his angry sister.

'You don't look much like a fine lady now,' he said scornfully. Her red hair was unbraided and was standing up like fire around her face, her grey-green eyes were blazing and sparking.

'Don't change the subject!'

'I'm not . . . its just that . . .'

'It's just that you don't know what to say! You've totally bungled the whole thing. Sir Kenneth will be coming here within the week and *nothing* is ready!'

'That is not true!' protested Neil.

'What am I to do? The girl is too ill to bargain with. I hope you don't think that I'll ride out on one of those horses!' She pointed scornfully at Neil's stocky Island charges innocently cropping the thin grass of the paddock.

'If Mairi will not part with the mare . . . you could ride out on Flame,' he said, wording it carefully so that it sounded as though he was offering a loan and not a gift.

'If she won't sell I'll *take* Flame . . . don't you think that I won't! But I'll never forgive you.'

'It's not my fault. At least I brought her here so that you could talk to her yourself . . .'

'Talk to her? The girl is delirious . . . possibly mad! She's saying all sorts of wild things in there . . .'

Neil went white and ran to the house.

'Come back here! I haven't finished speaking to you yet,' shouted Fiona indignantly.

But he had gone.

Inside the dim house he knocked someone flying as he raced to the room where Mairi was resting. Bursting in he found his mother standing on one side of her and Brother Durston on the other. She was propped up on a pile of rugs, her eyes open, but still with the abstracted, glassy look of someone with a high fever.

'Mairi?' he cried and flung himself at her, seizing her by the shoulders and thrusting his face close to hers. She showed no

59

sign of recognition or of alarm. Her head lolled like a rag doll.

'Neil, stop it at once! The girl is sick. What on earth do you think you are doing?'

'What has she been saying?' He looked at his mother furiously.

'The fever has been talking . . .'

'What? What has she been saying?'

Ingrid shook her head. 'Just nonsense. Fever talk.'

Brother Durston put his thin strong hand on Neil's arm. 'Leave us,' he said calmly, firmly. 'We have work to do here.'

'I won't go,' Neil said desperately.

'Neil!' his mother gasped, shocked at the intensity of his expression.

'It's all right,' Durston said quietly. 'He can stay and help me while you go and attend to the rest of your duties.'

'It's not fitting . . .'

'I need steam. He can fetch me hot water.'

'I'm not leaving her!' Neil said belligerently.

Durston looked at him sternly and Neil suddenly realized how foolish he was being. Whatever she had been saying was being put down to the fever. If he continued to make such a fuss they would begin to suspect that he wanted something kept hidden.

'I'll fetch the hot water,' he said hastily. 'Come mother – Fiona was looking for you.' How easy it was to lie once you started. Where would it end? He felt ashamed as he met Durston's eye. The hermit was not smiling. Neil followed his mother out of the room, thankful to have something practical to do that would keep him at least temporarily away from the shrewd monk. Ingrid went in search of Fiona.

When Neil returned to the room Brother Durston took the beaker of steaming water from him quickly and sprinkled some leaves into it, and then sat on the edge of the bed, gently holding the girl's head over the steam.

'Breathe deeply,' he said softly, commandingly. 'Deeply. Deeply.'

She did as she was bid. Neil could smell the spicy aromatic

steam from where he was standing and noticed that even as he breathed it in he himself began to feel calmer. He sat down on a little wooden stool that stood in the corner of the room, his shoulders hunched, his head sagging on his chest. He suddenly felt tired. He had acted on impulse in bringing the girl to his home and he was still sure that he had had no alternative. But now the future did not seem as simple as it had done at the moment of decision. He wished he could talk to Mairi and that she could understand him. She might not realize that she must say nothing of 'her people' and the Devil's Stones to his family. She might think that they would be different from her own villagers. Of course they would not stone her! Neil's lip curled with bitterness as he remembered the savagery with which the crowd had turned on her. But there would certainly be harsh things said and she might be treated warily and coldly. Maybe she would even be asked to leave. He would hate her to be hurt. She had been hurt enough in her short life. 'Her short life?' he repeated. How quickly he had forgotten the mysterious extension of her life into other realms.

When he looked up at last she was lying back fast asleep, breathing peacefully, and Brother Durston was looking at him with a thoughtful expression.

Neil stood up. 'She looks much better now,' he said. 'There is no need for you to stay.' The hermit did not move but continued to look at him steadily. 'I'll call you if she needs you,' Neil insisted. 'It's better if we leave her now to sleep.'

'You are right. Sleep is the greatest healer of all,' the hermit said and stood up. His head almost touched the ceiling of the low room. 'Will you walk with me?' he asked quietly.

Neil swallowed.

'I . . . I had better stay here . . . Just in case . . .' he stammered.

Durston nodded.

'I will not press you. When you are ready to talk, you know where I am.' He bowed slightly, and, with no further words, left the room. Neil stood looking after him, biting his lip.

Chapter 7

The Curse

The household was preparing for a wedding and however much Neil wanted to stay with Mairi he was forced to leave her side. He and Donal, his eldest brother, were in charge of the slaughter of the animals for roasting and they had to ride to the high pasture to fetch them down.

Neil was pleased not to have time to visit the hermit, knowing that if he did it would not be long before Brother Durston would have the whole story. On the other hand, to leave Mairi alone amongst strangers without having warned her to be silent was almost more than he could bear. Brother Durston, even if he did not approve of her beliefs, would protect her from harm from the others. He would not put it past his sister to treat her spitefully for no better reason than that she wanted the white Norman mare. As he rode a few steps behind Donal's sturdy Island beast he thought and thought about Mairi. He believed in the Devil and his dark friends as he believed in Christ and his angels of light. In the brief time he had known Mairi he had felt her to be on the side of light. Even the tall sinister Stones that had filled him with such fear at his first encounter had seemed benign in their strength when he had been with her. Not once had he sensed evil in her. Surely his deepest feelings could not be wrong. No, the people must be wrong in associating these Stones with the Devil. Surely they must be wrong?

Donal had been whistling cheerfully as he rode, and he now turned to look back at Neil.

'In love, brother?' he called cheerfully.

Neil flushed angrily.

'Of course not!' he answered sharply.

Donal chuckled and turned his attention back to the trail they were following.

'I've never known you so gloomy,' he shouted a little later, looking back with a grin.

'Is being gloomy a sign of being in love?' Neil shouted back indignantly.

'It's a sign of something.'

'Well, it isn't love,' said Neil firmly.

Donal laughed and rode on.

The deep peat underfoot was springy and squelchy. Even so high up they had to pick their way carefully. The hard rocky core of the island let none of the water through, and the rain that fell from the skies so frequently and so heavily had no-where to go but into the peat, or the lakes, or back into the sea in thousands of little trickling streams. To the right of them was the ocean, to the left the hills of the high pasture, and beyond them and further towards the southeast were the dark mysteri-ous crags of the Peaks where no one ventured except the eagles and an occasional intrepid hunter.

The cattle were found. Their thick shaggy coats had been shed for the summer. Neil had a twinge of pity for them as he and his brother selected three of the fattest and turned their heads back towards the farmstead. How horrible it would be to have no freedom of will, no possibility of making one's own decisions, of shaping one's own life. Difficult as it was to make choices and understand life enough to make the right decisions, at least humans had the challenge and excitement of trying. He looked at the backs of the three animals they were driving down the trail to their deaths and was thankful that God had given man a soul and free will – no matter how dire the consequences might be.

'Neil!' shouted Donal suddenly from behind him. 'Watch what you're doing. You nearly drove that beast over the cliff!'

Neil turned the animal with a shrill ululating call and tried to concentrate better on what he was supposed to be doing.

* * * *

Late in the afternoon Mairi woke from a deep and healing sleep to find a strange tall man sitting beside her, his face strongly grooved from years of ascetic living, his long-fingered hands folded quietly on his lap and his dark eyes fixed peacefully on her face.

She stared at him quietly for a few moments and he made no attempt to hurry her into speech. Neil had told her about his friend the hermit, and she felt sure that this must be he. She looked around the room wonderingly. This was no hermit's cell, but a room with a good comfortable bed and curtains of woven cloth hanging over the stone walls to keep out the cold. A room in a house grander than she had ever seen. Neil's house. She remembered their arrival, and a shadow passed over her face as she remembered the red-haired girl taking the bridle of Moon-Metal.

She looked into the hermit's eyes again.

'My mare?' she whispered.

'She is safe.'

'Neil?'

'He will be here soon. He has been sent on an errand.'

She felt no fear of her surroundings. She trusted Neil completely, and this was his friend.

'What do you call your mare?' Brother Durston asked gently.

'Moon-Metal,' she said dreamily. She was loath to wake fully, the bed wonderfully comfortable with so many rugs.

'That is a beautiful name. Is there a story to the choosing?'

'I was given her in the moonlight and she shone like silver.'

'Silver. Moon-Metal. That is apt.'

'It is a word my people use,' she said trustingly.

'Your people? Are you not of the Island?'

'Yes . . . now I am. There was a time . . .' A slight frown came to her brow as she puzzled how to explain what she meant. Her links with the distant past were so real to her she thought of them as unquestionably of the same order of reality as her present.

'There was a time . . .' he prompted.

'I was born here . . . now . . . and yet I came from over the sea . . . from the west . . . from . . .' She paused, suddenly aware that she should not be talking like this to a stranger.

'You mean your ancestors came from over the sea? The Vikings? But they are from the North and the East.'

'No,' she said slowly. 'Not my ancestors . . . not the Vikings. Myself . . . *I* came from the West.'

There was silence in the room. From the rest of the house faint sounds penetrated: Neil's mother calling to someone, chickens clucking in the yard as Fiona threw out grain for them, a dog barking on the hill behind the house as it spotted the figures of Neil and Donal and the three steers in the distance.

'You must tell me about your people . . . about your journey . . . from the West,' Brother Durston said at last, quietly.

Her face lit up. Neil had been right about the hermit. He would understand and help her.

'It is difficult to explain. In a sense I suppose they must be my ancestors and I am somehow remembering them by going to the place, the circle of stones, that was so much part of their lives. And yet . . . and yet . . . I feel . . . I see them around me as though I am one of them . . . although . . .' Again she stopped, and Brother Durston sat very still, waiting.

'Although . . .?' he prompted at last.

'Although I know this cannot be. Do you think that I am mad or a . . . or a . . .' She could not say the dread word her accusers had used so cruelly against her. 'Neil saw them too – in a dream – though he will not admit it now.' She looked into his eyes longing for reassurance. He thought he could see a recurrence of the symptoms of the fever. She had lifted her head and was straining to sit up. He put his hand to her shoulder and gently pressed her down again.

'You are not well enough to talk of these matters yet,' he said firmly. 'When Neil is back and you are stronger you must visit me, and we will sit and watch the sea and you will tell me about your people who came from the west.'

'Sometimes I am frightened . . .'

'When you see your people?'

'No, never when they are with me . . . only when . . .'

The door burst open and Fiona came in with a wooden bowl full of steaming broth.

'I am glad to see you awake,' she said briskly. 'Mother says you must drink this.'

She looked disappointed to see Brother Durston sitting beside the bed. She had been planning to settle the matter of the white mare without more delay.

He stood up, stooping to avoid the low beams.

'I was just about to leave,' he said, 'because I think she needs to be alone to rest.'

'Oh – of course – but she should have some food first.'

'Are you hungry?' he asked, looking at Mairi. Her eyes looked very big in her drawn face. The fever flush was returning and she looked extremely weak. She shook her head almost imperceptibly.

'I think you should try to have a little. We will help you.'

He reached out his hand for the bowl but Fiona drew it back.

'There is no need for you to stay Brother Durston,' she said hastily. 'I will feed her.' Fiona always felt ill at ease with the hermit and could not understand why Neil wanted to spend so much time with him. 'His eyes make me shiver,' she had confided to Donal once. 'I know what you mean,' he said, 'It is as though he hears what you are thinking and not what you are saying.'

Durston bowed his head slightly and started to leave. At the doorway he looked back and found Mairi's eyes seeking his appealingly. To Fiona he said: 'Help her with the broth, but then leave her to sleep. Tomorrow she will be stronger. Today she should think of nothing but of getting well.' Fiona sensed the command in the apparently mild words and bridled.

'You can trust me Brother Durston,' she said sharply. 'I have nursed sick people before.'

'Of course,' he said, and with one last look at Mairi, left the room.

Fiona smiled, relieved, and came to take her place on the stool beside the girl's bed.

'This is Neil's bed you know,' she said.

'Oh . . . I am sorry . . . where will he . . .?'

'Oh he will sleep somewhere or other. He is used to being moved around when we have guests.'

'I am sorry . . .'

'Don't be sorry,' Fiona said. 'I'm glad you are here. You must stay for my wedding.'

Mairi did not answer.

'I will be going to live in Scotia at the court of Prince David you know,' Fiona said.

Mairi nodded. Neil had told her this. She sipped the broth carefully.

'It is very important that everything goes well with this wedding,' Fiona continued. 'Sir Kenneth is used to very grand living. I cannot possibly go with him on one of our ugly little Island horses.' She looked hard at Mairi. 'I would be mocked by all the fine ladies and the lords at Court.' Fiona held the bowl of broth just out of reach of Mairi. Mairi shut her eyes and made no attempt to reach for it. Fiona leant forward a little closer, her eyes sparking dangerously. 'My father will give you a good price for the mare.' There was no expression on Mairi's face. She kept her eyes shut. 'And you would be allowed to choose any horse you want from our stock to replace it. We would not expect you to be without a horse.' There was still no sign from Mairi that she was even listening to Fiona's words.

Fiona banged the spoon impatiently back into the bowl, spilling some of the broth on the furs that covered the bed. 'After all it does not matter what horse *you* ride – *you* will not be living among princes!'

Suddenly Mairi opened her eyes and looked directly at Fiona.

'Moon-Metal was a gift. I cannot sell her.'

Fiona's face flushed with anger, but she kept control herself. 'These are special circumstances,' she said. 'I'm sure – whoever gave you the mare – would understand.'

'Moon-Metal is my friend. I cannot part from her.'

Fiona stood up angrily and dashed the bowl on the floor.

The broth spread out over the stone flags, chilling instantly, the fat congealing.

'Moon-Metal is a mare!' she shouted. 'An *animal*!'

'She is no ordinary animal.'

'That is why I want her!'

'And that is why I cannot let her go.'

Fiona was shaking with frustration and rage, and Mairi's face was very flushed. Her fingers were plucking nervously at the fur of the rug over her chest.

'You are ungrateful. We have saved your life – taken you in and nursed you – and yet you will not . . .'

Tears began streaming down Mairi's face.

'Please don't . . . please don't ask me for her . . .'

'I do ask you for her. I plead with you for her. Can you not understand how it would be for me to be riding such a horse when I arrive at the court of Prince David?'

Mairi sobbed and buried her face in her hands.

Fiona waited tensely for her answer and as the girl continued to sob and showed no sign of giving in, she shot her last arrow and it went home.

'You are the devil's child,' she cried, 'you have no heart! I saw the white mare in a dream and I saw myself riding it beside Sir Kenneth. Would God have shown me that vision if He did not intend it to come true?'

Mairi suddenly sat up and her face was wild and tear-stained.

'I am *not* the devil's child!' she screamed. 'Take it! If God meant you to have it – take it! But if you are lying to me about the dream . . .' and here her face was so contorted with hate and pain, Fiona went white . . . 'If you are tricking me with your lies, you will be cursed!' Her voice rose to a shriek on the last word and Fiona sprang back, horrified. Her foot slipped on the cold mutton fat on the floor, and she lost her footing, and crashed down on the hard stone. Her scream brought half the household running to her aid. When they came in they saw Fiona on the floor and Mairi half out of bed, leaning over her, her face as white as stone, her eyes filled with horror.

'Fiona?' cried her mother, rushing to her side. She narrowly missed slipping on the fat herself and had to steady herself against the bed. Fiona was screaming hysterically and making no attempt to get up. Her father who had followed his wife in to the room, saw at once the spilt bowl and the greasy skid marks on the stone. He held the others back with his arm and called for someone to fetch a broom and hot water. He then stepped carefully forward and helped his wife lift Fiona. No one took any notice of Mairi who had climbed out of the bed on the other side and shakily made her way out of the room and down the corridor . . .

When Neil and Donal returned to the farmhouse they found it in an uproar. They were told that Fiona had been cursed by that strange girl Neil had brought to the house and that her legs were now paralysed. Mairi had disappeared and some of the men were out hunting her, wearing every talisman against the evil-eye they could find.

Neil was horrified. This was worse than anything he had imagined. He could not believe that Mairi would curse Fiona and yet Fiona swore to it, claiming that her legs now had no feeling in them and could take no weight. She had tried to stand several times, helped by her family, but each time her legs had buckled helplessly beneath her. Witnesses had seen her on the floor with the girl leaning over her and the very fact that Mairi had run away seemed to confirm her guilt.

Neil's mother wept: his father looked grave. Brother Durston knelt and prayed beside Fiona who, exhausted from her hysteria, was lying pale and frightened on her bed.

Neil stayed at the house long enough to have three different versions of the tale told him by various members of the household before he rushed out to start his own search. There would be time enough to get the true story later, he thought. Now he must find Mairi before the angry men did. He was told that they had ridden in the direction of Glen Valtos, no doubt assuming that she would be attempting to return to her home village. They did not know as Neil did that she now had no home . . . except, and as this thought struck him, he frowned . . . she looked on the Devil's Stones as her home. He remembered how he had found her clinging to the tallest and how she had talked as though 'her people' were still present among the Stones and would help her. There was no reason to doubt that she would now return to them.

He rushed to the paddock to fetch Flame but on arrival found that Moon-Metal was beside him. It was inconceivable that she would have started back to Callanish without Moon-Metal: and if she were not on horseback she could not have gone far. Neil looked in the various barns and cattle byres, scoured the farm-yard and the rocky knoll behind the house. There was no sign of her. If she had made for the hills of the high pasture he and Donal would have seen her on their way back. Could she have made for the coast? The hermit's cell was at the top of a smooth green hill that overlooked the vast western ocean. One side of it dropped sheer to the rocky beach far below. Then there was the fishing harbour, a narrow cleft between cliffs to the north. Could she have gone there, thinking that a boat would take her away from yet another mob of angry people.

Was she indeed the witch her neighbours said she was?

And then he was angry with himself for doubting her. Her 'people' at the Stones were no more than the figments of the imagination of a lonely girl. She had a sensitivity, an intelligence greater than the people in her village. There was no one there she could talk to about the things that mattered to her. She was resented by her father because he had no sons, and mistreated by him. Neil himself understood something of what it was to be a misfit in his own community. He had run away to Iceland with a Viking trade ship when he was a child and had found the ignorance and insularity of his family and neighbours irksome when he had returned an older and a wiser person. Mairi had not travelled and seen other countries as he had – but she had ambition and imagination beyond her fellows. Her restlessness had to be satisfied by her dreams. No. She was no witch. She was like him – an adventurer cooped up in a restrictive and limiting environment.

He did not believe she had cursed or would curse any human being. Perhaps she had been lonely and afraid when she awoke and Fiona had taken advantage of this to pester her about the white mare. He could believe that they had an argument and because Fiona could not make her change her mind she had concocted the story of the curse. But why were Fiona's legs paralysed? Was Fiona pretending? It seemed inconceivable that even his headstrong sister would risk so much to get her own way. Her wedding day was approaching fast and there were a hundred matters that needed her attention. She could not afford to be incapacitated at this time. And why invent a 'curse'? What was it about Mairi that made people think in terms of demons and curses? There was nothing in her appearance or her nature to suggest this. Fiona had not heard of her connection with the Devil Stones. Was it possible that he was deluded . . . that she was . . .

But whatever the truth he wanted to find it out himself. He did not want to take the word of an ignorant and blood-thirsty mob.

'Mairi!' he called desperately. 'Mairi!' Gannets rose screeching . . . wheeling and squawking . . . He went to the edge of the cliff and looked over, fearful that it was on the rocks below that he would find her. But there was no sign of her . . . only the birds swooping and the sea breaking in long streamers of foam. He hurried to Brother Durston's hut, half expecting her to be sheltering there. But the hut was empty and dark, the hermit still at the house ministering to Fiona.

He searched everywhere he could think of and only returned to the house when it was too dark to see. The men were back and had found no sign of her on the road to Kirkoway. There was a great deal of talk of the devil having spirited her away.

Neil was questioned about her, but he was cautious in his replies. He insisted that Fiona must have misunderstood something Mairi had said. He would not believe that the girl had done what Fiona claimed. His father, who had kept his head remarkably well through all the excitement, lost his temper at last and demanded whether Neil was claiming that his own sister was lying.

'No, of course not. But . . .'

'But – what?'

'I know Mairi.'

'How long have you known her?'

Neil wanted to say 'since the beginning of time' because that is what came to his mind, but he stopped himself and said:

'Long enough.'

'And your sister?' his father demanded.

Neil was silent, thinking about his sister. He had lived in the same house as her since he was born and yet he knew her less than he knew Mairi.

'Let me speak to Fiona alone . . .'

'She is tired. We want her to sleep now.'

'If she is sleeping I will not disturb her. Let me just look in at the door.'

Neil's father would have been glad of an alternative explanation for the extraordinary events of the afternoon. He looked at Neil and told himself that if Neil did not believe the girl had done what Fiona had said she had done then there was some hope that it had all been a misunderstanding . . .

'Go then – but don't upset her.'

Neil rushed to Fiona's door. She was lying on her back on a pile of rugs, sucking her thumb as she used to do when she was a very young child. He slipped in and sat beside her. She was half asleep when he entered but she soon became alert and removed her thumb from her mouth. She looked at him accusingly.

'Fiona, what happened?'

'Have they not told you?'

'I have heard so many different stories I would like to hear the truth of it from you.'

'She is really an evil person, Neil. She cursed me so that I cannot . . . move my legs. Oh Neil, what am I to do? You must find her and force her to take the curse off me. You must.' Tears were beginning to fall.

Neil stroked her hand awkwardly, trying to think clearly, to speak carefully. He could see that she was still terribly upset and still determined to hold to her story.

'But Fiona – she's not evil . . .' He wished that the beginnings of a doubt about this were not creeping into his mind.

'She *is!* You should have heard her.'

'Tell me *exactly* what happened.'

'I brought her some soup. I was determined to be kind to her even though at first she refused to let me have the mare . . .'

'At first? Did she let you have it in the end?'

'We were talking about it and I . . . I told her how important it was to me and she suddenly screamed a curse at me and said that I could have the mare. She said that she did not want it any more. But what use is it to me like this? Neil – you *must* find her – you must make her take this curse off me. I'll even give her her mare back! I'd rather be dead than crippled. Sir Kenneth will never marry me like this!'

Neil's heart sank. There seemed no doubt that Fiona genuinely believed that she had been cursed and there seemed no doubt that she was genuinely paralysed. Dark thoughts about Mairi returned to plague him. What did he know of her after all? Was it possible that he had been bewitched by her beauty?

Donal had asked him if he was in love and he had denied it. But the thought of not seeing her again . . . the thought of her not being what he had believed . . . was agony. He turned away from Fiona and strode out of the room.

Outside in the cold, wild night she was wandering: lonely, misunderstood and afraid. Or she was with 'her people', triumphant and unrepentant. Which?

Chapter 8

The Sea Cave

At first light after a restless night Neil decided to visit Brother Durston. He had dreamt several times in the fitful intervals of sleep of the ceaseless pounding of waves against rock. It was as though the sea were hammering at his skull trying to get in. He struggled to wake each time, aware that he was dreaming even while he was asleep – almost driven to madness by the thud . . . thud . . . thud of the waves. He remembered what Mairi had said about dreams. These dreams had the same quality as the one he had had of Callanish and the tall feather-clad priest. Each time he woke he told himself it was only a dream, and each time he dozed off again he took up the dream exactly where he had escaped from it before.

He decided to tell Brother Durston everything he knew about Mairi and ask for his help. There was no point in hiding anything now.

The sky over the inland hills and mountains was beginning to glow as he set off, the farm buildings standing out against it in silhouette. Directly above him the sky was still blue-black. But gradually, with every moment that passed, it became more transparent, more and more a deep and translucent blue. Above the sea the most brilliant stars still shone.

He found Brother Durston kneeling at the edge of the cliff beyond his hut, facing the ocean and the last stars, his hands folded in prayer, his eyes shut. Neil stood behind him, his heart pounding from running up the hill. Whether the hermit had heard him approach or not Neil could not tell. He gave no sign.

Neil stood for a while impatiently behind him, expecting him at any moment to break off and greet him. But as time passed and Brother Durston did not move a muscle Neil remembered that the prayers of his friend were not like other people's – a long string of requests for the Almighty to fulfil – but were, as he had once told Neil, 'a going into the Silence where God's thoughts can be heard'. He had been known to spend a whole day or night this way without having noticed that any time had passed at all. Neil sighed heavily and flung himself down on the cold turf, prepared for a long wait.

At first he found his thoughts racing about in every direction, scraps of memory of this or that mingling with speculations about Mairi and feelings of resentment against Fiona whom, he felt, must have provoked whatever it was that Mairi had said. He thought about the storm in Glen Valtos . . . the strange tall Stones of Callanish and the even stranger crystal eye that Mairi had gazed into. Round and round all these thoughts and images went; many times expressed in the same stale sentences as though he were trying to hide from the meaning of what had been happening by clinging to the outer form of the words. But gradually as the sky lightened his breathing calmed, his thoughts slowed down, and he forgot everything, including himself. Birds winged overhead and he did not hear them. The stars were no longer visible, yet his eyes still stared at the point where the brightest had last been seen. Thinking back on it later he realized that he had never felt so peaceful . . . as though there were no distinction between himself and the sky and the earth and the ocean. His busy human mind was no longer the centre from which everything was viewed, but was only a small part of the awareness of everything. He felt what the sea-bird felt as he swooped over the water scanning below its surface for fish . . . he felt the fishes fear . . . he felt how it was to be water . . . to be air . . . to be earth . . . to be star . . . to be . . .

'Neil,' said Brother Durston softly and, startled back into his own limited consciousness, Neil stared up at the tall figure of the monk standing above him. He felt anger and frustration. He did not want to return to his own bag of skin and feel nothing more than that which he habitually felt.

Brother Durston smiled, reading his thoughts.

'To resent the return means that you have not understood the journey,' he said quietly.

What did he mean? Why must he always talk in riddles? Neil buried his head on his knees and tried to understand. It seemed to him that because everything in this magnificent and diverse universe sprang originally from one thought in the Mind of God and the One Word in which He expressed that thought we have a sense of Oneness with everything in this universe: an awareness that we all have a single destiny. Other Thoughts in the Mind of God might give rise to other universes, unimaginable to us, but ours is the one we know and the one in which we are inextricably bound together. Neil thought he understood now what Durston meant about the journey and the return home. He had gone a long way in his thoughts and had gained an understanding that must be brought back into ordinary life – otherwise there would have been little point in making the journey.

When he looked up again the hermit was sitting beside him and it was full light.

'When you arrived you were very agitated. What did you want to tell me?' Brother Durston looked at him with affection.

'So you knew that I was here all along?'

'Yes.'

'I thought that when you were in one of your meditations you were not aware of anything.'

Durston laughed. 'On the contrary,' he said. 'I am aware of Everything.'

Neil bit his lip. 'I meant,' he started to say, but Durston interrupted him.

'I know what you meant . . . and I think I know why you have come.'

'It is about Mairi.'

'I know.'

'I want to tell you about her and I want you to help me find her.'

'I too want to find her.'

'Before . . . before I talk about her – can I ask you some-thing?'

'Of course.'

'While I was waiting for you I . . . I sort of . . . slipped into what I think you must mean when you speak about 'the Si-lence'.'

'Yes.'

'I don't know how I did it. It just sort of happened.'

'At first it just "sort of happened" with me too,' Durston said with a smile.

'Did you have anything to do with my being there this time? Did you help me without my noticing it?'

'It is possible. "Being in the Silence" is a very powerful state to be in. My being there might have influenced you – but it would not have, had you not been ready for it.'

'Sometimes . . .' Neil frowned. It was so difficult to express those strange feelings and longings that he sometimes had that did not seem to belong to the 'Neil' that his family and friends knew. Durston could see that he was struggling and that he was not going to be able to say what he wanted to say.

'You were going to tell me about Mairi,' he prompted. 'You can do that while we have some breakfast.'

Neil stood up thankfully. He was hungry. Even brother Durston's oat cakes, hard and stale as they probably were, would be welcome.

Once having started to talk about Mairi Neil found it diffi-cult to stop. Durston listened quietly, carefully, occasionally asking a question. He heard things behind Neil's words that Neil himself did not realise were there.

When Neil at last came to describe the dreams he had had the night before of the sea beating into his skull Durston's ex-pression changed. He suddenly stood up and rummaged among the objects on his tiny shelf. He produced a long rope of hide-strips knotted together and, returning briskly to Neil, commanded that he follow him.

Puzzled, Neil stood up and was led back to the cliff edge. Then Durston turned and strode purposefully towards the north, skirting the drop to his left. They came to a place where the cliff was marginally less sheer and the edge was marked and scored from the ropes and feet of the local men and boys who for centuries had swung over the edge in search of guillemot eggs. Neil himself had gone over the rim on several occasions and knew well the thrill of fear as the icy winds pounced and plucked at the frail thread of rope, as the angry birds swooped and screeched, their eyes alien and cold, their beaks dagger-sharp. He frowned, watching Durston as he tied the end of his rope firmly to the rock they always used as anchor. Surely the hermit did not intend . . .? But before he could ask the questions that came crowding to his mind, the man had pulled up the skirts of his long, ragged monk's habit and had tucked them firmly between his legs and up into his belt. Neil stared with amazement at the long, thin white legs that were revealed. Durston laughed.

'I know it is many a long year since my legs have seen the sunlight,' he said cheerfully, 'but that does not mean that they are not strong.'

'You are not thinking of climbing down the cliff?' gasped Neil.

'I am going to fetch your friend,' the hermit said in a calm voice, as though it were a simple matter.

'You think she is down there?' cried Neil, surprised. It took a great deal of skill and daring to move about on those cliffs. If Mairi had gone over the edge it would be unlikely that she was still alive.

'Your dream made me think of that cave the sea crashes into at high tide,' Brother Durston said.

'But how could she possibly . . .?'

'She was frightened and desperate. In such a mood people do impossible things.'

Neil thought about the cave. He had been in it only once and that when he was about ten years old. He had been on an egg gathering expedition by himself – always a foolish thing to do – and had gone further and further until he had found that he could not get back. He had called and called but no one had heard him. At last, near nightfall, he had found a cave, above sea level but near enough for the water at high tide to thunder into it. He had spent a night of terror, crouched on a ledge deep in the cliff side while the sea tried to reach him and drag him down. He was shivering and exhausted by the time the tide turned and the blessed light of morning came creeping in. He had stumbled out and found to his relief that the cliffs were webbed with the swinging ropes of rescuers. He shuddered at the memory and wondered why he had not thought of that experience when he had woken from the dream. The memory of the cave that he had been trapped in as a child had undoubtedly fed and fuelled the terrors of his dream. Durston had told him that our thoughts are often in contact with one another – though we rarely consciously notice it. In moments of crisis or stress the contact is strongest. He had found Mairi once before as the result of a dream. Why not now? If she had been in the cave overnight and experienced its terrors, her thoughts might well have called to him, might well have reached him. He knew now what Durston was thinking and he knew also what he must do.

'It is I who must go,' he said to Durston, stepping forward and gripping the rope.

Durston pointed to the herb box tied to his side. 'It may be better that I go,' he said softly.

Neil hesitated. What if she were lying bleeding and with broken bones? But the hermit's thin legs looked as though they would snap as easily as kindling twigs against the rough rock. 'I'll take the box,' he said firmly. 'It would be better if you waited here.' Durston had taught him a great deal about herb lore over the years and he felt confident that he could deal with at least some of the possibilities that he might find when he found the girl. 'I could always signal if I needed you,' he added, fearing that he might be hurting the man's feelings by not believing that he was capable of the climb.

Durston was in fact much stronger than he looked and had been up and down those cliffs many times in search of his breakfast. However, Neil seemed so anxious to go alone that Durston agreed readily to stay behind, tying one end of the rope firmly around Neil's waist and taking up his position beside the rock that held the other end.

Seeing their old enemy the human-egg-snatcher coming, the birds went berserk, screaming and swooping around Neil's head. Sometimes he feared that they would peck his eyes out with their sharp yellow beaks, and he beat at them with his one arm, while the other clung desperately to the rock. Durston, watching him, said a fervent prayer to the guardian angels and hoped that his old hide rope would hold if it were called upon to take his full weight. He wished now that he had renewed it at the beginning of the summer as he had intended. He thought of throwing pebbles to chase away the angry birds, but feared that he might hit his young friend by mistake. He thought about the girl with the pale face and dark, deep eyes, the colour of the sky just before dawn, struggling to tell him about 'her people' from over the sea . . . from the west . . . He took his attention off Neil's plight for a moment to look at the vast reaches of the ocean that stretched away to the horizon. Legends spoke of land over that seemingly endless stretch of water. An Irish monk centuries before had claimed to have found it. The Vikings mentioned it in their sagas. Durston pondered what he had heard and saw no reason to doubt it. But believing that there was indeed land beyond the vast western ocean was one thing, and believing that people had come from that land in ancient times and raised the tall stones to their mysterious god in this island, was another. And then to carry it further and believe that a young girl now living could be in contact, across time, with such people – was asking a great deal of credulity. If Durston had not been a hermit but a monk living among other monks close to the constant supervision of the Church, he might have dismissed the girl's claim as at best ridiculous, at worst the influence of the devil. But as it was he lived alone on a stormy cliff, sometimes in the long winters not seeing another soul for months at a time, and his thoughts were often strange, his interpretations of what other people called reality often unusual. If he had learned anything in his long years of meditation it was that very little is as it seems, and there is much that is real that no one yet has a satisfactory explanation for.

Neil's mind was very active as he climbed down. On one level he was sharply aware of every possibility for grip and leverage among the cracks and crevices, and on another level he was detached from the immediate danger, weighing up the chances of the girl being alive and being in the cave.

When he had at last passed the nest level he was no longer attacked. His muscles ached as he stretched and clung, each foothold won with tremendous effort.

It had been easier when he was smaller. His present weight told against him and many crevices and notches he had used at ten were now too small for him. The girl was lighter than he was, but he still found it difficult to imagine her climbing down this cliff still weak as she must have been from the fever, and distraught from the harrowing experiences of the past few days.

When he could see the cave at last, a gash in the cliff side well above water level, which was now at low tide, he called her name. But sea wind blew it back in his face.

He strained to look up and could just make out Durston's head at the lip of the cliff. On the sea a few fishing boats were out, but they were far away and he was sure that they could not see him.

He moved nearer the cave and called again. But even at low tide the sea broke noisily on the rocks below, scattering fine spray into the air, and he realized that it would be very unlikely that the girl would hear his voice. That other time, long ago, he had not heard his father or his brothers calling as they combed the cliffs for him. On either side of him, and above and below, stretched the rich crystalline gneiss veined with crevices from which grew clouds of shimmering pink thrift.

His rope was not long enough and he had to loose it from his waist and make the last descent without it. He left it dangling, blowing from side to side, frail and thin.

At last he reached the cave.

In contrast to the bright sunlight, the blackness within the rock seemed absolute. He stood at the mouth and the memory of how he had felt all those years ago came flooding back. Fearfully he looked over his shoulder to check the height of the water. Was it lower or higher since he began his descent?

It seemed to him that it was almost on the turn and it took some courage to master his childhood fear of the place and stoop to enter. He stood in the darkness patiently waiting for his eyes to adjust to the change in light.

'Mairi!' he said loudly, and his voice boomed through the narrow corridors where the sea's voice usually thundered.

'Mairi!. . . Mai . . . Mai . . . ri . . . ri . . .'

'She is named after the mother of God,' Neil thought suddenly. 'Surely with such a name she could not be . . .'

Another name joined the echoes reverberating in the darkness. His own! Only a whisper at first, growing and mingling with the other.

She was there! She was there! He called again and moved deeper in. He could see dimly now. On one of the walls fine spider webs of light moved and flickered, reflections from a pool left over by the retreating tide touched by the thin ray of sunlight that beamed over his shoulder. He could see the ledge on which he had once crouched. He could see a dim shape moving.

He reached up his arms and – sobbing – the young woman fell into them. It seemed to him they kissed a hundred times. He was aware of nothing but the feel of her, the love of her, the longing to keep her close and safe. Whatever the past had been or the future would be, he would not part with her again.

Fiona lay all morning staring at the ceiling.

The joyful preparations for the wedding had given way to a full-scale search for the missing stranger, Fiona's parents knowing that the wedding would never take place if their daughter remained a cripple.

Donal had been despatched to Mairi's home village to bring

her back to lift the curse off Fiona at whatever cost. There was no doubt in anyone's mind that she would be trying to return to her home and, as she had not taken a horse and had not been seen on the road, it was assumed that she had chosen the hard way, through the mist-shrouded peaks, the haunt of the great golden eagle and the merlin.

Ingrid hovered over Fiona, frightened by the girl's stillness. Since her initial hysteria Fiona had lain without moving or speaking.

Her mother began to fear that the paralysis that had affected her legs was beginning to creep through the rest of her. She brought the girl's fine comb of walrus ivory and sat for a long while beside her bed combing her long red-gold hair. Tearfully she thought back over the years to when she had had to cajole and bribe Fiona to stand still long enough for her hair to be combed. The light shone and flickered in the bright tresses and the mother thought of her only daughter running to meet her brothers home from the high pasture . . . dancing in the great hall to the stamping and clapping of the neighbours . . . singing to the hens as she fed them grain. What if the spell could not be removed and she were crippled for life?

Suddenly she realized that the girl's grey-green eyes were looking into her own as though she had read her thoughts.

'Leave me mama,' Fiona whispered. 'Leave me alone.'

Ingrid's tears spilled over. Never in her life had Fiona been known to shun company. She had always delighted at being the centre of attention, attracting people to her as easily as the heather in full bloom attracted the bees.

At that moment one of Fiona's younger brothers appeared at the door.

'They think they have found her trail,' he said excitedly. 'We will soon have her!'

'May the Lord forgive me for what I am thinking I would like to do to her when I catch her,' Ingrid said with feeling, wiping her eyes.

'We will make her pay, Fiona!' the young lad said eagerly. 'Don't you worry. We will make her pay.'

'No,' said Fiona sharply. 'No!'

They both looked at her in astonishment. Ingrid bent over her daughter and kissed her. 'Bless you my darling,' she said, 'for your Christian charity and mercy. You will be rewarded in heaven.'

Fiona turned her face away from her mother and lay staring at the wall. There were things that she wished she had not done and had not said . . . but it was too late . . . too late . . .

'I wanted to die,' Mairi told Neil when she was calmer. 'I came to the cliff and thought I would jump off and kill myself. It seemed to me that everywhere I went, everything that I did, I was misunderstood. After what your sister was saying I did not think that even you would be my friend.'

Neil looked at her and felt ashamed. He remembered that he had in fact doubted her.

'But when I came to the cliff I could not jump. I wanted to live. I called to my people – but they did not answer. Then I really tried to jump. I thought that if they had deserted me too there was no point in living. But I still wanted to live. Can you understand that?'

Neil nodded. He understood wanting to live very, very well and remembered the times when travelling in Iceland, when he had thought his life was finished and how desperately he had clung to it.

'I decided to climb down. I thought I would leave it to the Great Spirit. If it was meant that I should die I would fall and break my neck. If it was meant that I should live I would some-how survive and find somewhere to hide.'

'And then you found this cave!'

'Oh Neil – the night . . . the night was so long!' She started to shiver at the memory and he put his arms around her and held her close.

'I know . . .' he said with feeling, remembering that other night years before. 'We must get you out of here before the tide turns again.'

'How did you find me?'

'I had a dream.'

'A dream?' Her eyes lit up.

'Yes. I will tell you later. But we must go now.' The water was already reaching into the mouth of the cave.

'But if you dreamed where I was then there is truth in my people and all that they have told me . . .' she cried eagerly.

'There is no time now,' he said sharply. 'Come.' And he took her arm and half dragged her to the entrance.

It was a miracle that she had climbed safely down the cliff to the cave and he prayed that a miracle would see them to the cliff top. He was relieved to see Durston waving vigorously. He had spotted them at once.

In full daylight Mairi looked very drawn and ill. Whatever strength she had had in daring that precipitous place the evening before had deserted her now. Durston's rope swung above them, out of reach.

Neil looked at her. Thin and small as she was he knew that he could not carry her and hold onto the cliff at the same time. He saw her look up at the towering walls above her and squint at the brilliance of the sky beyond Brother Durston's head. She bit her lip.

'You can do it,' he urged. 'It is not far to the rope. If I go first all you have to do is watch where I put my feet and hands and put your own in exactly the same places.'

She wiped her eyes on the back of her hand and he could see that she was fighting the rise of tears.

'You must not cry,' he said firmly. 'Because if you do you will not be able to see where the footholds are.'

She nodded and blinked and swallowed rapidly.

'Say a prayer,' he added more gently. 'Brother Durston swears that there are guardian angels . . .'

'I know it,' she whispered.

She shut her eyes and took a deep breath.

When she opened them again he had started towards the place where the rope was swinging in the breeze.

* * * *

At last, exhausted, they hauled themselves over the cliff edge and fell at Brother Durston's feet. He was sitting as still as stone, his back straight, his legs crossed, his eyes shut, deep in The Silence.

Neil touched Mairi's arm. 'I expect he was helping us with the climb,' he said. She was too worn out to speak but lay on the windblown grass and heather looking up at the sky. With each beat of her heart as it pounded in her chest she said the words 'thank you'. Thank you to the sun for its shining; to the rock of the cliff for its strength in holding firm under their weight; to Neil for finding her; to the strange hermit for holding them in the power of his prayer while they climbed; to the wind for not blowing too strongly; to the rope that did not break. But – above all to the Great Spirit her people had told her about, the Mystery beyond all mysteries, who had chosen that she should live and given her reason for living.

Durston opened his eyes and smiled at them.

Neil nodded, still unable to speak, his breath coming hard; but the man could see the gratitude and relief in his eyes.

He bent over the girl who had now shut her eyes. Her hands and knees were bleeding where she had torn them on the rock, her face was streaked with sweat and dust, her cheeks shadowed from her lack of sleep, but he saw God's child, no child of the devil.

He stooped and gathered her up in his long arms.

'Follow when you can,' he said to Neil. 'I will take her home and hide her until she is strong enough to face her accusers.' He had heard voices in the distance and feared that the people who were searching for her were headed towards them. She made no effort to hold on to him, but lay as limp as rag in his arms, her mind drifting helplessly like flotsam on the sea, touching a thought here and a thought there – but holding on to none. Somewhere in all that drifting a face formed in her mind's-eye and faded again. It was a face she had seen in her temple of the tall Stones. So they had been there after all, 'her people', and it had only been her fear and despair that had kept her from seeing and hearing them.

Durston laid her down on a pile of straw covered with a ragged blanket. He bulked so large in the small hut that his body hid the light that came from the doorway. The last thing she remembered as she fell into a deep sleep was the feeling that she was safe at last. The strength that she sensed in him seemed to her the same strength that she sensed in her ancient teachers and companions.

'Perhaps if he were to come to the Stones, he would see them too,' she thought – and then thought no more.

Chapter 9

The Healing

Having established that Mairi was safely sleeping in Durston's cell, Neil returned to the house. There was a hush over it; everyone moving quietly and talking in whispers.

Neil strode straight to Fiona's room and found her lying on her back, wide awake, staring at the ceiling. She did not even turn her head to see who had entered.

He stood beside her, looking down at her for a long while in silence. Apart from an occasional blink there was no sign that she was conscious. He could not believe that this shadow was his sister, who for years had been given her way in everything and had stamped her foot or tossed her red-gold hair if there had been the slightest hesitation in granting her wishes. He remembered racing her to the high pasture only a few weeks before and being hard pushed to keep up with her.

He had wondered how she would settle to being a court lady among pale women who talked of nothing but their husbands and their clothes, and had tried to persuade her to stay among her own people. She had always seemed to him like a wild, restless mountain stream, full of life and sparkle. It broke his heart to see her now, so still and passive – like a stagnant pool.

'Fiona,' he whispered. He could not bring himself to speak aloud in the oppressive silence of the room. She gave no sign that she had heard. He stooped closer to her and repeated her name a little louder. She still did not move. He put his hand on her shoulder and at last she turned her eyes to his. There was something in them he could not read. 'Is there anything I can do for you?' he whispered.

Her mouth twisted bitterly and her eyes seemed to say: 'Have you not done enough?'

'Fiona,' he said urgently, 'I really do not believe . . .' But he was not allowed to finish the sentence. His mother came bustling in and told him to let his sister rest.

'Where have you been?' she scolded. 'We have been looking everywhere for you. And that hermit too! We needed him and he was nowhere to be found.'

'I will fetch him now if you like,' he said, backing towards the door, wishing that he had never come.

'What do you think my darling,' Ingrid said to her daughter. 'Will you see him now?'

'No,' said Fiona in a cold, hard voice that Neil had never heard her use before.

'She refuses to see him,' Ingrid said with a sigh. 'I am sure his prayers will help. If the witch is not to be found to remove the spell, surely such a holy man would be able to do *something?*'

'I will fetch him whether she wants to see him or not,' Neil said.

'I will not see him,' snapped Fiona.

'You seem to *want* to stay crippled and miss your wedding!' Neil said impatiently, angrily.

'Neil!' gasped Ingrid, horrified.

Fiona's lips tightened and her eyes returned to the ceiling. Neil turned on his heel and left.

He took some food from the kitchen and a soft fur rug from one of the beds – and set off for Durston's cell.

In the hut Neil found that Durston had kindled a small fire in the central hearth and Mairi was sitting on the bed propped up against the wall. She was clutching an earthenware beaker full of water in both her hands and, bright-eyed, was talking animatedly to the hermit. As Neil entered Durston held up his hand, indicating that he should not interrupt. Neil sat quietly down on the hard floor beside him and listened.

'It first happened when I was very young. My father had taken me with him on his pony to trade with another farmer.

We were supposed to be collecting some sheep from him in exchange for a steer, but the sheep had strayed and we had to go in search of them. We found them near Callanish, but a lamb ran away and I followed it. I lost sight of my father and the lamb, and came suddenly upon those tall, tall Stones. I was shocked. So many! We had a single standing stone near our village and I had always been told to keep away from it because the Devil had put it there. This used to puzzle me because the sheep and cattle always used it as a back-scratching post, and I knew animals always shy away from something they sense is supernatural or evil. But I kept away because my mother said I should. When I found those others I stared and stared and longed to go up to them, but did not dare because of what I had been told about the one near our village. I went back to my father and he helped me find the lamb. I don't know why, but I didn't mention what I had seen to anyone. I thought there must be something fearful and secret about the Stones because I had never heard them mentioned, although they were not all that far from Kirkoway.'

She took a sip of water and Neil handed her some cold meat and bread from the bundle he had taken from the kitchen. She ate hungrily. And so did he.

'And then I started to have dreams about it,' she said.

'What kind of dreams?' asked Neil, remembering his own.

'I dreamed over and over again that I was lost, wandering about over the moors, frightened and not knowing in which direction lay my home. And then suddenly I would see the Stones against the skyline and know that *that* was my home. It was very strange. When I was looking for my home in the dream I always thought of it as it is, a cottage in the village with my mother and my father and the chickens . . . but when I *found* my home in the dream it was always those Stones standing up on that hill . . .'

'Did you go back to it. I mean . . . when you were awake?'

'Not for a long time. The dreams frightened me. I felt wicked even thinking about the place when I had been told that such Standing Stones were always the work of the Devil. And then it was as though . . . as though a gate had been opened . . .' She seemed to be struggling for the words, 'and all the thoughts I had ever had came rushing out as though they had been penned up in some paddock and were now free. My parent's explanations for things no longer satisfied me. It was as though the things that had made sense to me before suddenly no longer made sense, and the things that I had never understood became clear.'

Brother Durston helped himself to some of the food and munched quietly, saying nothing but listening closely to every word.

'One day I crept away on my father's pony and decided the only way to find out the truth and stop the dreams happening all the time, was to go back to the Stones themselves. I knew the way to the farm where we had traded the steer for the sheep, but after that I expected to have trouble finding my way.' She paused and frowned, thinking back. 'But I went straight there. It was very strange.'

'And then . . .?' prompted Neil as she showed no sign of continuing.

'It *was* as though I had found my home,' she said. 'I felt happy and at peace there . . . After that,' she added after another pause, 'I visited them every time I could manage to slip off without being noticed.'

She was silent for a while and Neil and Durston sat very still, waiting, knowing that there was more to the story.

'Nothing in particular happened in those days, but about a year ago everything changed.' She leaned forward as though aware that she had at last reached the really important part of her tale. 'I had noticed a black crystal in the tallest stone but had not thought it was anything special. Suddenly it began to look like an eye in the middle of a forehead, an eye gazing out over the loch and the islands. I stared and stared at it and it seemed to me that once I had started to stare at it I could not stop. I began to feel very strange, as though I would not be able to move even if I wanted to.'

'And could you?' Neil asked breathlessly.

'I don't know. I was too afraid to test it out. I just stood there gazing into the Eye and it seemed to me the light around me changed. The Stones seemed much whiter, the black crystal more and more like an eye. It had been a cloudy day but now there was sunshine blazing off the Stones. I could feel the presence of people around me, but I could not stop looking into the 'eye' to see if they were really there. I knew that they were not our local people. I knew . . . I just *knew* that they were my people and that they were from the ancient, ancient past.'

'Ghosts?' whispered Neil.

'No. Not ghosts. Real people like you and me but without . . . without their bodies.'

Neil was silent.

'I heard voices speaking in a strange language. I strained to understand what they were saying but the words were very different from the ones I was used to. I gave up trying to hear and just went on staring at the Eye. And then a bird flew past and screeched and I looked up startled. I was alone as before among the Stones and it was starting to rain. I tried to stare back at the Eye . . . but this time nothing happened. I went home – very confused.' She paused a long time. 'After that – every time I went to the Stones and looked into the Eye something happened. I began to understand the language. I began to see the people. They spoke to me directly and told me all sorts of things.'

'What – what did they tell you?' cried Neil eagerly.

'Sometimes they told me things and sometimes I just saw pictures.'

'Did they tell you where they came from?' Durston suddenly asked in his deep voice.

'They talked of a land far, far across the western ocean. It seemed that in the ancient days there had been two brothers, two great chiefs. The Great Spirit had breathed wisdom into two tablets of stone and given one to each brother. The two brothers looked at the tablets and could not see the wisdom in them. The Great Spirit then told them that one day they would be able to see it – but first they must follow his instructions. One must stay where he was in his ancestral lands, keeping his tablet safe, living according to the ancient laws of his people, while the other brother was to take his tablet and his tribe and move towards the east. He was to keep moving towards the sunrise, learning everything that there was to learn on the way. When the time was right he must return and put his stone tablet next to that of his brother. Then and only then would they be able to see what had always been there. The new knowledge and the old joined together at last to illuminate the true wisdom.'

She stopped speaking and sat with her hands in her lap, very quietly.

After a long time Neil took a deep breath and looked at Brother Durston.

'Does that sound to you like a tale the Devil would tell?'

Durston shook his head very slowly, deep in thought.

'They told me the journey would take a long, long time because man is slow to learn and easily distracted. They showed me the strange little ships they came in . . . they showed me how they had spread across the land . . . building the sacred circles of their ancestors, setting up in each place tablets of stone in memory of the one they guarded containing the breath of the Great Spirit . . . carving on rock the spirals representing the spirit journeys of their people . . .'

'That priest I saw with the great crown and the cloak of feathers . . .?' Neil asked wonderingly.

'That was the High Priest. Birds are sacred to them because they fly from the earth and sing in the sky, the place of the Spirit. The priest clad himself in feathers to show his respect for the bird's wisdom. Wrens sing around his head as he walks the processional way because the birds know of *his* wisdom.'

'And you?' asked Brother Durston. 'How is it that you can see them and talk to them while no one else can?'

'They say I was chosen as "a carrier of the message" because I had special gifts. They say that in each age someone is chosen to know the story . . . so that the people will not forget the journey back when the time comes.'

'What are the "special gifts" that you possess?' Durston asked with interest.

'I have always . . .' But here the girl hung her head and looked almost afraid to continue. It was only the encouragement she saw in Durston's eyes that made her resume. 'I have *sometimes* had dreams that told what was about to happen . . . and *some-times* I can tell what people are thinking . . . and once . . . I saw an angel.' She looked at Durston nervously, wondering if she had gone too far and he would at last be shocked and angry.

'Tell me about the angel,' he said quietly.

'I saw it by the altar in the church – quite clearly.'

'What did it look like?' Neil asked, awed.

'Like light . . . shining . . .'

'Did it say anything?'

'It told me that my grandmother was dying, but that I must not worry because 'in God's kingdom she will live forever'. And then . . . and then it was gone.'

'And when you came home,' Durston said. 'You found that your grandmother had died?'

'Yes. The villagers were very angry when I tried to tell them about the angel and said that I was a wicked girl and that I lied. It puzzled me. The priest is always talking about angels as though they really exist. If they do – why is it so impossible that I had seen one?'

Durston shook his head thoughtfully.

Neil suddenly remembered his sister. He jumped up with an exclamation. 'Fiona' he almost shouted. 'I promised my mother I would bring you to her!' he said to Durston. 'She thinks you might be able to . . .' and then he stopped, remembering that it was supposed to be a curse from Mairi that had crippled his sister. He looked at the girl, confused, thinking about all the strange things that she had been telling them. 'They are look-ing for Mairi,' he added awkwardly, 'because they think that she put a spell on Fiona and that she is the only one who will be able to remove it.'

The light in Mairi's face went out. Talking to people who listened without judging too hastily, she had forgotten the rest of the world.

'I will go to your sister,' Durston said calmly and stood up.

As he stooped through the door he looked back at Neil. 'Look after her,' he said with such loving concern in his voice that Neil felt confident that Durston had no doubts she was innocent of all that she had been accused. He felt ashamed that he himself had once again, even momentarily, lost faith.

There was an awkward silence between them for a short while after Durston left, which Neil broke at last by asking if 'her people' had told her how the travelling 'brother' would know when it is time to return with the stone tablet.

'When we have learned the new wisdom properly and know how to use it without distorting and corrupting it, we'll be ready to return. But if we return without understanding, we could bring about death and destruction rather than the golden age prophesied.'

Brother Durston was greeted nervously by Fiona's mother.

Her attitude to him had always been ambiguous. She was awed by him because he was a holy man and lived so closely in communion with his God, but his appearance had always frightened and sometimes disgusted her. His immense height and his extreme leanness, his hollow cheeks, his penetrating eyes . . . all disconcerted her. She knew that her son Neil played chess with him and she indeed admired the beauty of the little chess pieces he carved out of walrus ivory and the wise precepts Neil often learned from him. But the fact that he lived all through the long winter in his tiny smoky hut of stone and emerged like a scarecrow dressed in blackened rags as the sun returned did not endear him to her tidy house-wife's heart. She was relieved to see now that he must have recently washed and appeared in clothes almost acceptable to her. As he stooped through the doorway she thought she could see something of the man Neil almost hero-worshiped and was ashamed that she had ever tried to intervene in the friendship between them.

Brother Durston strode to Fiona's bedside and stood looking down at her for what seemed a long time. Then he turned to Ingrid hovering at the door and nodded as though to dismiss her. She retreated, disappointed. She had hoped to watch the holy man at work, half expecting to see a demon fleeing dramatically from her daughter. But it was clear that he wanted to be alone.

With many an anxious backward glance the mother left the room.

Fiona knew that Brother Durston was beside her, but she refused to look at him.

'Fiona . . .' he said, after a long silence.

'Why did you come?' she said harshly. 'I told mother that I did not want to see you.'

'And why did you not want to see me?'

'There is nothing that you can do for me.'

'How do you know that?'

'I know,' she said stubbornly; but Durston noticed that her lip trembled slightly before she thought to stiffen it again.

'You know because you know what has caused your crippled legs.'

'Yes.'

'It was not Mairi, was it?'

'Of course it was Mairi!' she answered sharply. 'It was the curse she put on me.'

'The curse *she* put on you?'

'Yes.' She looked at him suspiciously. 'Why do you say it like that?'

'Question yourself. Not me.'

Fiona pursed her lips angrily.

'Go away. I am tired. I have to rest.'

'You will have no rest until you can walk again.'

'Then I will never rest again!'

'That is your choice.'

'Oh Brother Durston!' She suddenly changed her mood and tears came rushing to her eyes. 'I would give anything to be able to walk again. Anything!'

'You will walk again when you can face the truth about yourself,' he said quietly.

'What do you mean?' she said tearfully; but deep inside herself she knew what he was trying to say.

There was silence between them for a few moments.

'If I am to help you,' he said at last, mildly, 'I have to know exactly what happened.'

'Did mama not tell you?'

'I want to hear it from you.' He was looking at her steadily and she found that she could not look away.

'I brought her some soup.'

'The soup was spilled. How did that happen?'

'She knocked it out of my hand . . .'

Durston said nothing, but continued to look into her eyes.

'All right,' she said at last and flushed. 'I was angry and threw it on the floor.'

'*You* threw it on the floor because you could not control your anger?'

'Yes,' she said bitterly, ashamed.

'The fat in the soup congealed on the cold stone floor and made it slippery.'

'I suppose so.'

'What happened then?'

'We were talking about the horse and I told her how important it was for me to be properly mounted when I rode to Prince David's court.'

'Why?'

'Because . . . is it not *obvious*?' she said impatiently.

'Not to me.'

'I did not want to shame my parents.'

'Your parents would not be shamed if you did not have an expensive Norman horse. Jesus rode into Jerusalem on a donkey. Was he shamed? Were his parents shamed?'

'Oh – you do not understand!' she cried, exasperated.

'I think I do.'

Fiona's face was red and angry now.

'At any rate,' she stammered, 'whatever you may think, Mairi understood and said I could have the horse.'

'It seems odd that she should curse you if she had willingly agreed to give you the horse.'

'It was after I told her about the dream I had about my riding the white mare to meet my bridegroom.'

'You had such a dream?'

Fiona bit her lip. There were two bright red spots on her cheeks and her eyes would not meet Durston's.

'Well – I did not actually have it. I made it up to persuade her to give me the horse. It was just a little story. It did not hurt anyone.'

'Did she believe that you had had the dream? Was that why she said you could have the mare?'

'Yes.'

'Was it such a little lie? You were using one of the great mysteries of the human soul – the gift of divination by dream – making a mockery of it as a demon or a charlatan would.'

Fiona looked horrified.

'No . . . no . . . I did not mean . . .'

'If we use these mysteries to cheat our fellow man he loses trust in them . . . and then a precious and valuable gift from God is spoiled and wasted.'

Fiona was sobbing.

'I never thought of it like that . . . I never meant . . .'

'Did she believe you? Did she?'

'Yes. Yes . . . well, I don't know. She said if I was lying I would be cursed . . .' She suddenly realized what she had said and stopped with a gasp.

Durston who had been stooping over her straightened up and squared his shoulders.

'As I thought,' he said shortly. 'Stand up! There is nothing the matter with you.'

'But . . . but . . .'

'You slipped on the fat which you had thrown on the floor in anger. You slipped because you moved without care – again in anger. You hurt your back as anyone would falling on these stone floors. Fear and guilt did the rest. Stand up.' he commanded.

'I can't!' she sobbed.

Suddenly he stooped and hauled her up by the arms.

'No, I can't!' she screamed. 'I can't!'

For a moment impatience and anger suffused his own face, and then he took command of himself and let her fall back on the bed.

'I'm sorry,' he said. 'You see I do understand very well how easy it is to lose one's temper.'

He drew a stool up beside the bed and sat upon it.

'Let us sit quietly together,' he said in a gentler voice. 'We both have work to do upon ourselves.' He shut his eyes as though he were praying and she tried to join him but she could not – too many other things were whirling around in her head. All day she had lain, unable to move her legs, convinced that she was crippled for life. She had told herself the story of what had happened a hundred different ways – determined to put the blame on Mairi and on no one else. But as fast as she told the story, something deep inside her that would not be stilled, rejected it and led her back to the original version, the one she did not want to face. Now that Brother Durston had forced her to face it another whisper had started in her head. If she could walk again she would have to leave home where she was blindly loved to live among strangers who might judge and condemn her. Brother Durston had shown her something in herself she did not like. Would others see it?

He opened his eyes and looked at her. Pity filled his heart for the misery he saw in her face. He took her hands in his.

'It is all right,' he said softly. 'It is all right. All is made new. You can walk.'

'I . . . do . . . not . . . want . . . to!' She forced the words out, trembling uncontrollably, terrified that she had spoken words to a stranger from so deep in her secret heart. He put his arm around her and held her against his shoulder, trying to comfort her, thinking gravely about what she had said.

He did not ask her why she had said what she had. He waited, knowing that when she was ready she would tell him, and once she had told him she would be half way to recovery.

'I am afraid . . .' she whispered at last, and he had to bend his head towards her to hear her voice.

'What are you afraid of?'

'I am afraid of . . . getting married . . . going away . . . every-thing! I think I am even afraid of myself.'

He stroked her head and said nothing.

'Are you not going to tell me not to be afraid?' She asked in surprise, looking up and feeling much calmer.

'No. I cannot tell you that. Courage is something you have to discover for yourself.'

She frowned.

'You see,' he said. 'Already, from just having told me, you are less afraid. And from just having realized your own nature, you are half way to conquering it.'

'I am not sure I understand.'

'What do you want most in all the world at this moment?'

'To have courage . . . to be someone Sir Kenneth will love . . .'

'You see! Yesterday what you wanted most in all the world was someone else's horse!'

She laughed. It was as though the heavy dark cloud that had pinned her to the bed had lifted like magic. Without thinking about it she sat up and swung her legs over the edge of the bed. Durston stood up quickly and took her arm.

'Now – let us go and see how the wedding preparations are progressing,' he said cheerfully.

She followed him without a backward look.

Chapter 10

Donal

In the early afternoon Donal had to abandon his own horse because he had ridden it so hard – the poor beast was near to collapse. He had found a farmer who knew and respected his father and was prepared to lend him a horse until Donal returned the following day, on the understanding that he would swear to treat it with more consideration than he had his own.

Donal accepted food and a brief rest in exchange for the story of how his brother had brought a guest to the house who had put a crippling curse on his sister. The farmer and his wife and their wide-eyed children hastily crossed themselves and then, when they heard from which village she had come, they told a few highly exaggerated stories of their own about how a terrifying storm had raged the night of her birth, and how a neighbour's flock of sheep had walked straight off a precipice after she had looked at them.

Donal was urged to continue his journey with no further delay, his saddle being transferred to the borrowed horse by the son, while a smacking kiss was planted on his cheek by the daughter. Fervent wishes of Godspeed rang in his ears from all of them as he galloped away, leaving them with another tale to tell against Mairi.

When he at last reached Kirkoway it was growing dark and he was greeted by a pack of barking dogs. One of the cottagers came out, armed with a club, to see who was causing the commotion. He stood at his doorway, scowling, and watched Donal ride slowly towards him, the dogs circling angrily around his horse's legs, but keeping just out of range of his boot.

'What is your business?' the surly man asked as Donal came level with him. He took the lamp from his wife who had followed him out and held it close to the horse's head. The beast shied away uneasily. The cottager gripped his club menacingly.

'I know this horse – it belongs to Iain of Gisla,' he said suspiciously.

'That is true,' Donal said hastily. 'He is a friend of my father and has loaned it to me for a day and a night. My own horse was worn out and is in his safe keeping until I return.'

From every cottage in sight men and women and children were emerging. He looked at their sullen and suspicious faces and felt uneasy. His own family was wary of strangers, but never treated them with such hostility. One of the dogs had gripped his boot heel and was snarling and tugging. He lifted his leg suddenly and the cur went flying, howling and whimpering to its master. More men appeared and surrounded him angrily.

'I am Donal, the son of Lorn of Uig. The wife of Iain of Gisla is called Kirsten, their children Alastair and Morag. Would I have this knowledge if I had not supped with them as a friend?'

The stony stare of the crowd did not soften.

'Yes,' someone said, 'it is possible to sup with a man and know the names of his family and still leave him for dead and steal his horse.'

Suddenly a thickset man, who had been in the background, came forward. 'The son of Lorn of Uig?' he asked.

'Yes.'

'What is your brother's name?'

'Neil,' he said.

It was obvious that the man recognised the name. The others stood back a pace or two, as though they now acknowledged that whatever business Donal had was a matter for the surly, thickset man who had recognised his family name. But they did not move away.

After a long, uneasy silence, Donal decided to act as though nothing was amiss.

'Is it possible as son of Lorn of Uig, and as brother of Neil who is known to you, I might find lodging for the night?' he asked, boldly.

No one replied, and Donal was just beginning to wonder what he should do next, when a woman stepped forward and announced that he would be welcome in her house.

His relief was shortlived, however, when he realised the woman was the wife of the man who had asked his brother's name and was now glowering at him with extraordinary suspicion and dislike. But, as there did not seem to be any alternative, Donal thanked her and moved to follow her.

The others, content now that someone had taken responsibility for the stranger, began to disperse, but not without many a whisper and a dark backward glance. The dogs made one last frantic attempt to frighten him and then gave up and slunk after their masters.

Braden, with an ill grace, showed him where to tether his horse and where the water and the hay was, and then led him into the dark and smoky interior of the cottage that was his home. There was no sign of anyone except his wife who was now stirring the cauldron that hung from the centre over a peat fire. She kept looking at Donal with anxious eyes. She seemed a nervous creature, very much under the domination of her husband. If he had not suspected it before, he would have known now who they were. The woman, though worn out by the hard life she led, was handsome, and through the wrinkles he could see something still of Mairi's extraordinary beauty. The place was neat and orderly and though small compared to Donal's own home, not unpleasant. In a corner were two beds with rough curtains half drawn over them.

He was given food and ale and ate and drank in silence, watched resentfully by the man, and fearfully by the woman. At last Braden demanded an explanation of Donal's visit.

As the time had gone by Donal had become more and more unsure of the best way to approach the subject. He had thought, when he was riding over the wild heather moors and skirting the swamps and the lochs, that he would gallop into the village and demand the parents of Mairi deliver the girl to him, or at least give him some kind of satisfaction for what she had done. He had not been clear in his mind as to what exactly he meant by this, but he had hoped that the girl was with them and could be forced to return with him. This would certainly be the most satisfactory end to his quest. But due to his weariness and the peculiar hostility of the villagers he found himself on the defensive.

He took a long swig of ale, partly to give himself time to think of his reply, and partly to give the impression that he was not in any way to be pressured against his will.

'I am looking for your daughter,' he said at last, meeting Braden's bold stare with one of his own.

Skena, the girl's mother, gasped. Her expression, uneasy before, was now desperately anxious. She looked as though she were about to speak, but Braden held up his hand and she fell back silent.

'And why are you looking for my daughter?' Braden demanded.

Donal decided to meet aggression with aggression.

'She has cursed my sister and I am looking for her to remove the curse.'

For what seemed a long time the two men stared at each other, tensely, as though each was waiting for the other to make the next move.

Suddenly the woman could bear it no longer. She flung herself forward, weeping, plucking at Donal's arm. 'It is a lie! It is a lie!' she cried. 'Mairi would curse no one. Whoever said she did – lied. Everyone lies about her.'

Braden suddenly hit her hard across the mouth and she went reeling back. Donal stood up shocked, clenching his fists. Braden was standing now too, facing him, the jug of ale fallen over and the liquid trickling to the floor.

'The woman is the witch's mother. She will say anything to protect her,' he said coldly.

'And you are her father,' Donal said. Horrified as he was at what Mairi had done, and angry as he was, the man's ugly act against his wife and daughter appalled him. He knew his own father, no matter what his children had done, would stand by them against an army of strangers.

'She is no child of mine,' the man snarled. 'The Devil spawned her and the devil can have her!'

Donal looked, startled, at the woman. She was cowering back, wiping the blood from the corner of her mouth. She did not deny the accusation, but then it would have taken superhuman courage to do so with her man in such a mood.

'But you brought her up. You are responsible for her,' Donal found himself saying.

'For that God may make me pay to the end of my days – but I will answer to no *man* for the deed I did in good faith. She deceived me,' he indicated his wife with a bitter thrust of his hand. 'She told me the child was mine. I was fool enough to believe her though it was born before time, only seven months after our marriage vows.' Braden began to pace up and down angrily muttering, half to himself. 'You would not think it now,' he said, 'but she was beautiful once – the most beautiful girl on the Island. I swear it. As innocent and young as a kitten. Or so I thought!'

Donal looked at the woman. Was she too a witch? Like Mairi, her face was clear of guile, her eyes though dark with sorrow and suffering, still as innocent as a kitten's. Donal looked back at her husband. It was *his* face that was twisted and distorted with hate, *his* eyes that were wells of suspicion and bitterness.

Braden was still muttering. 'They twist you and turn you, these women,' he said, 'until you go against your own instincts. I should have thrown them both out years ago when I first learned that the girl was a . . .' He did not complete the sentence, but went on glowering and pacing, the monologue continuing silently in his own head.

Donal stepped across to Mairi's mother and lifted her face to see how badly the blow had damaged her mouth. He noticed that she had other scars.

'Do you know where Mairi is?' he asked her in a low voice.

Something like a spark came to her eyes, and she drew back from his touch.

'I do not – and if I did I would not tell you. She is no witch.'

'I will not harm her. I just want her to help my sister.'

'She never hurt your sister. I will swear to it.'

'Maybe not. But I would be happier if I could at least talk to her about it.'

'She is not here,' Braden suddenly interrupted fiercely. 'Your brother probably knows where she is. Ask him!'

'He does not. He sent me here to find her.'

'The people tried to stone her,' Skena whispered, her face drawn with pain at the memory. 'Her friends and neighbours . . . only your brother, a stranger, tried to help her.'

'And for thanks she cursed his sister!' Braden snarled.

'Perhaps she did not,' Donal said frowning. 'Perhaps my sister was mistaken.'

'She cursed her. Have no doubt of it. She is the Devil's child. She visits him in his temple, and rides his cursed horse.'

Donal looked at him.

'The horse you tried to sell my brother?'

Braden pursed his lips at this and was silent.

'Yes, the horse he tried to sell your brother,' Skena said maliciously. Her husband turned a fearsome look on her but did not strike her again. Donal suspected that she would pay for that remark later – but for the moment the man held back, not sure if Donal would oppose him or not. Braden was a big and burly man but Donal, who had been three times wrestling champion of his district, was by no means an opponent to be taken lightly.

'The mare was a good one,' Braden mumbled. 'It was the girl . . . going out all hours of the night to the Devil's Stones . . .' Donal turned to Skena.

'If I swear I'll not harm her will you tell me where I can find her?'

'I have not seen her,' Skena said sadly. 'She has not come back here. I believed she was safe with your brother.'

'Is there any woman of the village she learned her witch spells from?'

'The women of this village are god-fearing, all of them,'

Braden said indignantly. 'If she learns any spells it is at the knee of the Devil himself in his temple on the hill at Callanish.'

'Where is that? Perhaps she is there now.'

'You take your life in your hands if you go there. It is a cursed place.'

'I am desperate to help my sister. I'll risk anything,' Donal said.

'It is back along the road you came.' Skena spoke before her husband could. 'You turn to the right when you see the mark-stone for the Dunfallen farm. You will see the tall stones against the sky before long. It is there she found the horse.'

'It is there she meets the devil,' growled Braden.

'I will pray well and truly before I venture there. But first I must sleep. I have no stomach to beard the Devil in the dark.'

Braden grunted and turned his back on Donal. Skena hurried forward and picked up the spilt jar and began mopping up the ale.

'You are welcome,' she said. 'You may sleep in . . . you may sleep in that bed.' She pointed to where her daughter used to sleep.

'Thank you,' Donal said and he lay down wearily and closed his eyes. For a long time he heard Braden pacing the room, occasionally muttering. But at last all was still.

When Brother Durston returned to his hut both Neil and Mairi were asleep, but as soon as he touched the door the girl woke with a start, and by the time he had entered she was crouching at the far side of the hut, the blanket drawn right up over her head.

'It is only I,' he said gently. 'You may come out of hiding child.'

Mairi peeped over the edge of the blanket and on seeing that it was in fact the hermit, emerged fully.

'How is she?' she asked at once, anxiously.

He smiled. 'She has recovered.'

Mairi buried her face in her hands and whispered fervently:

'Thank God. Oh thank you Lord God.'

Neil sleepily opened his eyes as Mairi flung her arms around him and shook him. 'She is better!' she cried. 'She can walk!'

And then as the thought struck her she looked at Brother Durston for confirmation. 'You did mean that she could walk again?'

He nodded.

'She is completely recovered?'

He nodded again and smiled. This time Neil hugged Mairi.

'I think you should go and see her,' Durston said. Mairi's face fell, remembering the bitterness of their last encounter.

'Not yet,' Neil pleaded. 'Surely she should stay here a while longer until she is really strong again. I will go and make sure she'll be welcome.'

'She will be welcome,' Durston said with conviction.

'What happened?' Neil asked. 'How did you remove . . . I mean how did you make her better?'

'She was not really crippled after all. The shock of the fall only made her think she was.'

'And when I think what they have been saying about Mairi!' Neil said angrily. 'I'll make them apologise . . .'

'No . . . please . . .' Mairi pleaded.

'Too much has been said in anger Neil. It is all best forgotten,' Durston said. 'There is a wedding to prepare for. Joyful things to think about.'

Neil looked at Mairi questioningly.

'He is right Neil. I want no apology. I spoke in anger too, and am ashamed.'

'Well, if you think . . .'

'I *do* think . . .'

Neil accepted this but still thought that he would prefer to go back to the farm by himself first to make sure that everything was as peaceful as Brother Durston said it was. The hermit was amused at his insistence but raised no objection.

After he had left there was silence in the close little cell for a while, the two people left behind avoiding speech rather than having nothing to say to each other. Durston folded up the blankets and Mairi busied herself packing up the chess pieces that Neil had been showing her and returning them to the little carved box of olive wood from the Holy Land – touching each piece with reverence, noting the skill with which it had been carved out of walrus ivory, wondering at the delicate lines of graining in the olive wood and whether the Lord himself had once rested in the shade of the tree from which it was cut. Perhaps he had sat with his back leaning against its trunk. She wondered if he missed his time on earth – whether he felt homesick for the sea of Galilee and the sunshine on the hills of his homeland as she felt homesick now for the ancestral lands of 'her people'. She knew that heaven must be a very wonderful place but . . . there was something about being alive on this earth . . . She had thought of this at the edge of the cliff when she had considered casting herself off. She had thought about it in the night as she crouched on the shelf in the cave terrified that the tide would not turn before it reached her. Her people had told her that we cling to earth because we can imagine nothing else, but that when we leave the earth we *change* and our desires change with us. The adult does not crave the toys the child finds so desirable, nor do we, when we are pure spirit, want what we wanted so badly when we were flesh and blood.

'Brother Durston,' Mairi suddenly said.

He was now sitting cross-legged on the floor, his hands quietly folded in his lap, not watching her directly, but being aware of her every movement, almost her every thought. She sat down opposite him feeling the urge to speak, to question, to be answered. She leant forward and looked into his eyes.

'Do you think,' she asked, 'that those people . . . my people really exist and . . . and really talk to me?'

He did not reply at once, but she could see that he was thinking deeply about the question.

'That I cannot say at the moment,' he said at last, slowly. 'There are so many different kinds of reality . . . so many mysteries in life . . . so many ways of experiencing things and of knowing things. There *are* Beings who exist in ways unimaginable to the human being. Most of the time they go their way in

the many mansions of our Lord . . . but sometimes they penetrate our world . . . by mistake or design . . . who knows . . ..
and Time seems to have no relevance to them . . .'

'You are a man of God, a Christian, and yet you do not say that they are the Devil's fiends as father and his friends do at home?'

Durston looked very thoughtful.

'God did not come into existence at the birth of Jesus Christ on this earth. God always existed and the ancient people had many names for what they could not understand but felt to be Divinity.'

'Sometimes I fear . . . I dread that I am what they say. How can I be sure that my people were listening to the true God?'

'Tell me what they have told you?'

Mairi looked at him in dismay. These people had been speaking to her for a long time and had influenced her whole way of thinking. She had never thought of putting their teaching into words for another person to understand. Where should she begin?

'It . . . it is difficult.'

'Try.'

'They talk about the Great Spirit . . .' She paused – wondering if Brother Durston would accept this as another name for his own god.

'Go on,' Durston said encouragingly.

'This Spirit is represented by a circle because everything is contained *within* the Great Circle of the Spirit.'

Durston nodded, but said nothing.

'They believe everything is linked. There are invisible spirit paths to every living thing . . . and they say everything is living – because everything is *part* of the Great Spirit.'

She looked at him anxiously – but he did not seem shocked.

'The first thing I learned from them was how to deliver prayer-feathers.'

'Prayer-feathers?'

'Yes. Each feather for a particular prayer. I was given several to deliver to different people and to different places. I was told to notice everything on the journey. One of the feathers I had to deliver was to a child who was very ill. I told no one what I was doing because I didn't want to be called a witch again. I just laid the feather on the child's chest without anyone noticing.

'When I returned to my people they questioned me about everything I had seen: what birds I had seen flying and in what direction – the direction of the wind and the water-flow in the streams – what reflections I had seen in the meres – which plants had been flowering, which seeding and which dying. And last of all what I had felt in my heart as I looked into the eyes of the child.'

'Perhaps it was just their way of training your powers of observation and your memory?'

'It was more than that. They believe the universe in harmony resonates with the Great Spirit . . . that each and every thing has its own theme within the Great Theme. When a minor theme is 'out of harmony' with the whole there is dis-cord, dis-order, dis-ease, and we experience this as suffering. The ritual of the prayer-feather, by encouraging our awareness of the place of everything in the Great Theme, helps us to re-establish the harmony. Something in the child's life was in discord: the food she ate, those around her anxious or fearful . . . *Something* was not as it should be. When I looked into her eyes and she into mine, the peace I felt – due to the sense I had of the harmonious wholeness of everything – helped the healing power of the Great Spirit to flow through me into her.'

'Did the child recover?'

'Yes,' she said joyfully.

They were silent for a while, each experiencing the beauty of what she called the 'Great Theme'.

Then she began to speak again, finding it a comfort to be able to speak freely about 'her people' at last.

'Sometimes I saw – in a sort of vision or dream – a person being put in an underground chamber. It was round, a bit like this hut, built of stone. He would be left there for a long time – the entrance sealed up. At first he sat quietly, and then he would be agitated and I would see him scratching at the walls trying to find the stones that had been put in last. When he couldn't he would sometimes weep and beat his head against the rock. But after a while he usually calmed down and stationed himself at the very centre of the circle, cross-legged on the floor, his eyes closed. At the end – when they at last let him out – they dressed him in special clothes with a magnificent feathered head-dress. Then the drumming and the dancing began. I longed to join in! The climax of the ceremony came when he stepped onto the burning embers of the fire and, with his arms and face raised to the sun, began to prophecy.

'Once I tried to walk on our peat fire at home,' she said. 'But I burnt my feet badly,' she added ruefully.

'The soul of the man you saw sitting in the chamber,' Durston said quietly, 'had left the world as we know it and was on a difficult and dangerous journey. Only his body remained behind – the shell, the shadow . . .'

Suddenly, to Mairi's horror, he put his own hand into the small hearth fire in the hut, and brought it out totally unscathed.

He smiled at her astonishment. 'You see it is not only your ancient people who know that the spirit is stronger than the body. But,' he added, 'there are many different ways of proving it. Sometimes just helping someone when it is inconvenient for you to do so is enough.'

She accepted this with a sigh. But it was so much more exciting to walk on fire!

Then he told her that her ancient people had wisdom – but she could not return to their ways and to their time. She had to 'pull their wisdom through to the present day' and use what was still relevant – still true. 'Remember the tablets of stone,' he said, 'the old and the new. What is good in each illuminates the other.'

'I remember,' she said.

He smiled, and quietly made the sign of the cross on her forehead. And then, after a slight hesitation, he enclosed it in a circle.

* * * *

While Durston was questioning Mairi about 'her people' and Donal was confronting her parents, a ship bearing Fiona's bride-groom was approaching Uig. A fine breeze filled its sail and the oarsmen were soundly sleeping. A young man paced the small wooden platform that served as a deck and stared at the stars. It was a year since he had seen the girl who was to be his bride and he was wondering if he had made a mistake. The islands were wild places and the people there, even those of the 'better' families, were uncouth compared to the Normans and the Norman influenced courtiers that he was now used to living among. His friends had advised him to forget the girl and make a marriage to advance his career among one of the several el-egant French ladies invited across to England by King Henry and now moving north to the Scottish courts of Alexander and David. He had thought of doing so on several occasions, but had hesitated so long that, each time, the young woman he was considering became betrothed to someone else.

Now in the night in the middle of the ocean Kenneth ques-tioned himself about these hesitations and knew that they had been not so much because he loved Fiona but because he loved his wild and rocky homeland. He had grown up in the Western Isles before the Norwegian king, Magnus Barefoot, had an-nexed them. Fiona's family was of proud native Hebridean stock, a family that had stood up against the enclosures of the Norse earls before Barefoot. As a young man Kenneth had crossed the sea to the mainland and become part, first of King Alexan-der's court and then of Prince David's in Cumbria. He had been one of the young attendants at Alexander's coronation at Scone, and his blood had raced to hear the Gaelic bard speak the gene-alogy of the king, like a mighty surging poem, running back to the ancient days, to the times before memory. He had been ex-cited to see the sacred stone on which kings had been crowned for centuries. Some said it was the very stone pillow on which Jacob had laid his head when he dreamed of the ladder between earth and heaven on which the angels ascended and descended. Others said that it was the Lia Fail brought from Tara in Ireland by their ancestors – the magic stone of pagan times that had cried out in acknowledgement when a true king stood upon it. No king could hold authority who did not take his vows upon it, nor trust to the loyalty of his earls who had not bowed the knee before it.

Kenneth had been a young boy when he had seen the king crowned, heard the prayers and the singing, seen the gathering of the proud chiefs of the great families. His heart had stirred then for his own people, his own heritage, and resentment against the Norsemen who ruled the North lands and the Western Isles, and the English and French who pressed upon them from the south, had stirred in his heart.

He had visited Lewis with a deputation from David's court and had seen Fiona of the fiery hair swirling to the old tunes, dancing until everyone else was exhausted, singing the high, weird Gaelic songs that told of the sea and the rock and the free flying birds. He had asked for her in marriage and had been promised. He had dreamed of her through the long year among the soft-spoken foreigners and yet now . . . now he was afraid.

The wind rose higher and the little ship heaved.

'How long?' he asked the captain and was told that this night and most of the following day would have to pass before they would reach their destination.

Could he go back? Could he go back in this way to his roots? Or had living abroad spoiled it all for him?

Durston and Mairi talked long, long into the night, while Neil rejoiced with his family over Fiona's recovery.

In Kirkoway Donal slept restlessly in Mairi's bed and on the hilly peninsula the tall Stones of Callanish stood as they had stood for millennia, witnesses of a people who believed that man would only reach true peace when the circle was completed, when the wanderer had returned and the ancient knowledge and the new illumined one another . . .

Chapter 11

The Reconciliation

By the time the dawn came it was raining, and Donal set off on his journey with the grey clouds so closely pressing at his back that he soon developed a sinking heart and an oppressive feeling of fear and gloom. When he reached the place where an ill-worn track led off to the right and he knew that it must be the one Mairi's mother had told him about, he paused, and then moved on, deciding to abandon his search for the girl. But he had not gone far before he reined in again and turned back. He owed it to his family to do everything he could to rescue Fiona.

At first there was nothing to see but clouds of rain driving over bleak moors, the sea and the islands lost somewhere in the mist. And then, suddenly, grey giants loomed out of the grey air and a chill that was colder than the rain's chill made him shiver.

He moved forward cautiously though he longed to leave the accursed place. He was not sure what he expected . . . but the place was deserted . . . grey . . . silent . . . empty . . . The Stones seemed to him to be sentinels . . . waiting . . . guarding . . . What was it that Mairi found there? Why did she keep coming back?

He dismounted and walked forward, climbing the hill, pausing at the entrance to the processional way. He felt drawn to walk the avenue to the central circle, but he resisted the urge.

He skirted the Stones cautiously, keeping his distance. He stopped finally at a point on the western side, the grey sea loch and the grey islands behind him, a line of grey Stones ahead of him leading to the central circle. Facing him was a tall thin Stone that seemed to be the centre-piece of the whole, the dominant 'presence'. Fearfully he looked at it. In the centre of its 'forehead' was a black 'eye'. He gasped. The impression that he was being looked at was very strong. He wanted to leave at once but he found that he could not draw his own eyes away from it. It seemed not so much to be looking *at* him, but *into* him. It seemed to be seeing all that he was and all that he had ever done. Its very silence made his own mind appear noisy with words and he found thoughts crowding into his mind that he had worked to suppress . . . the conceit he had for his prowess as a wrestler . . . the time he nearly killed a man because he wanted his wife . . . all that he had ever done that he was ashamed of seemed to be drawn to the surface and exposed by that implacable stare. He had to get away!

He started running, stumbling over half hidden boulders and tufts of heather, convinced that the great Stone had turned in its ancient socket and that the 'eye' was still looking at him. When he reached his horse he scrambled onto its back and urged it away from the place at a gallop, hardly taking notice of the potholes and pitfalls of the trackless heather-covered hills. The icy rain drove into his face and confused him even further. He made no attempt to think what route he was taking and had no idea that he was moving further and further away from the well trodden road that would take him home.

Suddenly his horse stumbled and lurched and Donal slithered off its back, almost disappearing into a cleft half covered by heather bushes and sedges. He swore as he clung to the tough bushes and fought for footing on a protruding rock. But luckily the arms that had made him champion wrestler had the strength to haul him up again to the surface unharmed.

He was about to stand up again and find out how his borrowed horse had fared when a glint of something in the cleft caught his eyes. He tugged back some of the branches and looked down into the darkness. Faintly he could see something . . . he was not sure what. He almost decided to leave it where it was, but curiosity got the better of him. By dint of ripping some of the heather bushes right up and away from the lip he let more light into the dim regions below. At first he found it difficult to decide what he was looking at, and then as his eyes grew more and more accustomed to the poor light he realized with horror that he was staring at a dead man, a skeleton still clad in the remains of a red cloak, with a studded belt around his waist and a sword at his side.

Donal pulled back away from the sight and took a deep breath in the clear rain washed air. Now, what should he do? Leave the body where he had found it and pretend that he had never seen it? Or bring it up to the surface and take it back to the village for Christian burial? He could not have been a local farmer. Perhaps a Viking or a Viking's victim from the days of fire and war? It was impossible to tell how long the man had lain there.

Donal was very tempted to leave him. The rain had increased in ferocity and he longed to be at home. The man had obviously been there a long time, a little longer would not hurt him. On the other hand the sword . . . Donal found himself crouching at the lip of the cleft again, peering at the sword. It was a good one. Even from this distance and with rust already at work on it he could see that it was a much better sword than any he had ever seen before.

Should he take the sword? But to rob a dead man . . .? He looked over his shoulder . . . grey veils of rain were driving across the bleak landscape . . . water was running over him, below him, around him . . . there was no sign of a living being in any direction apart from his horse, standing hunched and patient against the rain. Would it be robbery? The owner had no need of it now. How would he explain it at home? He had found it. That was no lie.

Before he had made a conscious decision he found himself scrambling down into the cleft, struggling for foothold on the slippery, water soaked sides, clutching rocks and roots. By the way the skull was lying it seemed that the man had broken his neck in the fall. Donal swallowed hard and tried not to look into the eye sockets as he carefully disengaged the sword. The belt and the other clothes were half rotted through and fell to pieces in his hands. But there was a dagger he had not seen from above, as grand as the sword. He tugged and pulled until he had both sword and dagger in his hands, and then, as fast as he could, the two weapons tucked into his own belt, he struggled out of the place, whistled to the horse, mounted and rode away.

Neil managed to persuade his family that Mairi had nothing to do with Fiona's temporary paralysis. Fiona admitted that she had been so shocked when she fell on the greasy floor she had mistakenly thought the stranger must have cursed her. Now she was sorry she had maligned the girl and asked her family to do all in their power to find the girl and to ask her forgiveness. Neil admitted to knowing where she was and set off at once to fetch his beautiful young friend from Brother Durston's hut.

Having at last found someone who would listen to an account of all the strange things that had happened to her without condemning her, Mairi had fallen contentedly into a deep and restful sleep. When Neil came for her she was looking a great deal better than he had seen her at any time since the storm in Glen Valtos. She was still a little pale, but there was now no question of fever or of fainting.

At first she was shy to go with Neil, fearing that the family still held her responsible in their hearts for what had happened to Fiona. But with both Brother Durston and Neil persuading her that this was not the case, and Neil passing on to her a message directly from Fiona herself that she was most welcome, Mairi was finally convinced.

Rain clouds were rolling in from the sea and the waves were wild and choppy in the wind. Neil looked at them somewhat anxiously, remembering that Fiona's bridegroom was somewhere on that sea. They had received word that he was coming by boat along the west coast of the Islands, instead of directly across the Minch and then overland to Uig. He could arrive any day now, and as far as Neil was concerned the sooner the better, before anything else went wrong.

Before they went into the house Mairi insisted on going to the paddock to see Moon-Metal. The mare was overjoyed to be reunited with her mistress and Neil stood aside, sheltering under the overhang of a haystack, watching while the two nuz-zled and fondled each other – Mairi whispering lovingly to the silver creature – Moon-Metal whinnying softly as though try-ing to tell the girl how much she had missed her.

Neil wondered what was to happen now about the mare. Fiona had not mentioned her since her dramatic recovery and no one else had dared to bring up the subject. He hated to think of Mairi and Moon-Metal being parted. On the other hand he hated to think of himself losing Flame, and he knew Fiona was quite capable of holding him to his offer of Flame if Moon-Metal was not to be hers.

'Come,' he said at last, anxious for the two girls to meet and the matter to be resolved. Mairi came, but with a long and lin-gering look back over her shoulder to Moon-Metal. The mare tried to follow but the dry-stone wall and the gate prevented her. She stood forlornly looking after them, her chin resting on the top row of the stones.

Fiona was found surrounded by the women of the household trying on the fine clothes that she would be wearing for the wedding. Simple homespun would not do for such an occasion and cloth had been bought from a trader, a fine silk brocade the like of which had hardly been seen on the Islands, though com-mon enough now in the English court.

Fiona was laughing and turning in circles for the admiring crowd to notice how the fabric shone and changed colour with her movements. Her eyes were bright and her cheeks flushed with excitement. When she caught sight of Mairi standing in the doorway beside Neil she stopped at once and went a little pale. The two girls stared at each other for what seemed to Neil to be a long time. He could not see Mairi's face as he was be-hind her, but Fiona looked uncertain of herself. Suddenly she dismissed the women.

'Come in,' she said to Mairi. 'Come in and see my dress.'

The others left, some still smiling and chattering, some look-ing sideways at Mairi as though they still suspected her of occult powers. Neil pushed in beside Mairi, determined to be there to protect her if she needed it.

'You, my brother? I have never known you to be interested in a new dress,' said Fiona, amused.

'It is not the dress that I am interested in,' he said.

'Out! Out with the rest,' Fiona commanded. 'Mairi and I have things to settle between us.'

Neil could see Mairi's frightened face. He did not want to leave her alone with his sister but Fiona was determined that he should. 'Leave us!' she repeated sharply and Neil found himself leaving. Long years of having her own way had made Fiona forceful.

He met Mairi's eyes.

'It's all right,' she said quietly. 'It is better that we are alone.'

'If you are sure . . .' he muttered feebly and left as she gave a reassuring smile.

Outside the door he was swept up by a deputation of his younger brothers with messages for him to come and attend to the animals.

The ship on which Sir Kenneth was a passenger was battered by the waves so mercilessly that it lost its course and lost time. The Captain now said that they would not be able to make port before nightfall . . . possibly not even before the following day. Sir Kenneth both cursed and blessed the delay, still not being at all sure what he wanted of the future.

Brother Durston knelt in his dark and smoky cell and prayed for guidance, feeling in his bones that what Mairi had told him had the ring of truth about it, yet wanting to be sure that she had been in touch with an ancient and god-fearing priesthood, and not just mischievous and misleading spirits from the dead.

Donal hid his newly acquired dagger and sword when he went to take back his borrowed horse and reclaim his own.

He refused hospitality and hurried on his way, strapping his new weapons proudly to his belt as soon as he was out of sight.

Left alone, the two young women looked at each other for a long while before either spoke.

It was Fiona at last who made the first move. Without speaking, but with tears in her eyes, she held out her arms to Mairi. The girl ran to her and for a moment or two they clung together, both asking forgiveness of the other.

'No, no it is I who must be forgiven,' said Fiona. 'I had no right to press you so hard about your mare. You had every right to refuse me. But most of all – I had no right to say those terrible things about you to my family.'

'It is I who must be forgiven,' Mairi interrupted. 'I spoke in such bitterness and anger, and should never, never have said what I did.'

'You did not curse me. I cursed myself by lying. Brother Durston showed me that.'

Mairi smiled, relieved. And then they stood looking at each other again, awkwardly, not quite knowing what to say next. It was Mairi who cleared her throat and spoke at last.

'I . . . I would like you to have Moon-Metal as a wedding present,' she said in a low voice. Fiona could scarcely catch what she was saying, but she heard enough to know that her dearest wish had been granted. She could hardly believe it and her eyes shone. She saw herself again as she had before riding to meet Sir Kenneth as grand as any Norman lady.

'You are indeed a friend!' she cried. 'There could not be a better gift!' And then, seeing Mairi's face, she knew in her heart that she ought to refuse to accept such a sacrifice. But she could not. 'You must come with me,' she said impulsively. 'Yes. That is the solution! You must come with me when I leave and then you will always be near Moon-Metal. You will be able to exercise her when I cannot and take care of her when I am too busy.'

Mairi looked startled. Across the sea! The thought terrified her . . . and then she remembered that she was homeless and that in this new life Fiona was offering her no one would call her a witch. That would be good. But she would have to leave the Tall Stones and 'her people'. That she did not want to do. Her face fell.

'I'm sorry . . .' she murmured.

'No!' Fiona cried. 'It is all settled. You are coming!'

'I really cannot leave . . .'

'Nonsense! You will have a wonderful time. You will meet all sorts of handsome young men – far more handsome than my brother Neil – and wear clothes as fine as this every day . . .'

'That is not . . .'

'I *will* not hear another word! We will be the greatest of friends and you will be as happy as I am.'

Mairi was silent at last. She felt almost suffocated by the girl's sudden, overwhelming affection, as she had been before by her hostility.

Chapter 12

The Bridegroom

During the early hours of the following morning the rain petered out and from headland to headland beacons blazed out to greet Fiona's bridegroom.

In the great hall all was finally ready for the celebration, the tables scrubbed, new straw on the floor. In the kitchen the cooks were preparing the feast. The tired kitchen boys sleeping on the flagstones, dreaming of cauldrons and steam and knives amongst the greasy smells, were shaken awake. Mountains of feathers plucked from ducks and chickens occupied a corner, an old skin thrown over them to keep them from drifting about with every draught. Ingrid had wanted them kept to stuff a mattress, but had not intended that they should stay in the kitchen. Someone would receive a sharp word no doubt when they were discovered. All along one side of the kitchen, from the rafters, the meat and game hung ready for roasting, dripping into a wooden trough. On the other side were the bundles of dried herbs. Barrels of homebrewed ale and a neat row of jars containing imported wine for the most honoured guests, stood ready. Beside the hearth, slabs of peat were neatly stacked to keep the great open cooking fire perpetually alight.

Fiona insisted that Mairi should not leave her side and the two girls were now in one bed. The bride-to-be slept heavily, her red-gold hair tousled on the pillow beside the unruffled sloe-black of the younger girl. Mairi lay sleepless on her back staring at the square of window through which at first the rain had buffeted its way, and now, silently, the stars peered. She had never known a house with a window before and was thinking how wonderful it was, an eye to look out on the world while you stayed protected inside. If she went with Fiona there would be more wonders than this. But if she went with Fiona she would be separated from her people and her home – and by this she did not mean her parents and her village. She knew that she would never be able to talk to Fiona about the things that really mattered to her. She would be cut off from the source of her real life and be condemned to living a half-life like most other people. She would have to leave Neil. Would he want her to go or to stay? His feelings towards her seemed so ambiguous. One moment he was tender and caring, and then, just when she was beginning to feel certain that he loved her, there was that look of doubt that crossed his face – that withdrawal, that barrier. He did not really understand her. Would he ever? Should she stay for him and face the hurt time and again of that dark and questioning look?

She thought about the way Fiona had not let her out of her sight all day; the way she had asked for her opinion on every detail of the wedding; the way she had talked about what they were going to do together in the new country . . . At first she had felt almost suffocated by the attention and wished it would stop. But as the day wore on Mairi began to realize that Fiona was afraid – afraid of the marriage – afraid of the journey into a strange country to live among strangers. She had never had a sister and no doubt had longed for one. In Mairi she saw a chance of having someone with her from her own country – a sister – a companion. Mairi's quietness deceived Fiona into thinking that she was docile and pliable, ready to be moulded into anything Fiona wanted. She knew nothing of the extraordinary extension of Mairi's life. The very intensity of her early hatred and resentment of her, swung to the other extreme because Fiona was in such a state of contradictory emotions. She longed for Kenneth and marriage – and yet she feared both. She longed to leave the constrictions of her parent's home, yet she feared to leave its protection.

When the Scottish ship was finally sighted off the headland, a deputation to meet the young lord was quickly on its way.

Ingrid stayed behind to supervise the last moment arrange-
ments, but her husband rode with Fiona at the head of the party,
Neil and Mairi close behind them.

When the time had come for Fiona, rather than Mairi, to
mount Moon-Metal, there was a moment of awkwardness. Neil,
seeing the expression in Mairi's eyes, had taken her hand and
squeezed it sympathetically. She turned her head into his shoulder and swallowed hard, trying not to cry. Moon-Metal herself
tried to come towards her former mistress, but Fiona, her colour high and bright, her back straight, her stiff brocade half
covering the mare's silver flanks, reined her in and turned her
head firmly to the path towards the harbour. The little procession was ready to go.

Neil lifted Mairi's chin and looked anxiously into her eyes.

'It is all right,' she murmured. 'I want her to have Moon-
Metal. Brother Durston explained about how wrong it is to want
to possess something so badly that you would sin to keep it.
My anger was a sin. My words . . .' her voice trailed away at
the shame she felt for the ease with which a curse, albeit ob-
lique, had come to her lips. 'Moon-Metal came to me when I
needed her,' she said. 'Now – Fiona needs her.'

He bent his head and kissed her lips. He held her by the shoulders. He wanted to hold her closer still but his name was called
and they drew apart. He rode away beside his father, calling to
the dogs.

Mairi reached for the reins of the neat little brown mare that
had been allotted to her and followed him with a sigh.

Donal arrived back too late to set off with the welcoming party.
He rode into the yard with a clatter just after the last figure had
disappeared over the brow of the hill. His mother bustled out to
meet him, chiding him for being late.

He looked astonished.

'I have been all the way to Kirkoway and back. Do you not
want to hear if I found the girl or not?'

'What girl?'

'The girl Mairi. The witch.'

'Oh Mairi,' said Ingrid impatiently. 'We found her. She is no witch after all. They have all gone down to the harbour to meet Sir Kenneth. You should be there too. But clean yourself up a bit before you go,' she added disapprovingly, looking at his mud spattered clothes.

'And Fiona . . .?' Donal asked, bewildered.

'She is fine. I told you, the girl never put a curse on her. But there is no time to talk about it now. You, as Fiona's eldest brother, should be there . . .'

'I am not so sure she is not a witch. I went to those Devil's Stones of hers and . . .'

'Fiona is perfectly all right now. Brother Durston has assured us that she had nothing to do with Fiona's accident . . .'

'But I tell you – those Stones she goes to *are* bewitched.'

For a moment she was shocked out of her state of busy distraction. 'You went to some Devil's Stones?' she cried.

'Yes.'

'Donal!'

'I was looking for her. Her parents had not seen her – and you *did* send me to find her!' He sounded aggrieved. He had come home full of stories to tell and there was no one to listen to him. 'Where is she now?'

'She is with Fiona. Oh the Lord preserve us! She and Fiona are as close as sisters. She even plans to go with her when she leaves for the Mainland! What am I to believe! What *am* I to believe?'

'It seems to me very odd how quickly everything has turned around since I have been away.'

Ingrid wrung her hands. 'What shall we do?'

Donal thought hard. At her parent's home he had been convinced that she was innocent. It was only when he felt the weird power of that crystal 'eye' that he had changed his mind.

'Ride after them Donal. See that she does no harm.'

He nodded and moved to mount his tired horse again. But she called him back again and told him to change his clothes and wash his face.

'Quickly,' she cried. 'Quickly!' She was not sure if Mairi was a witch or not – but she was sure Fiona would be shamed by a brother who looked as dishevelled and dirty as Donal did at this moment.

While he was inside obeying her she told the stable boy to rub his weary steed down and give it fresh water to drink.

When he emerged at last in his best clothes, clean and almost neat, a magnificent and unfamiliar sword and dagger at his side, her pride in him almost made her forget her anxiety for her daughter.

Neil, waiting on the cliff top above the small inlet that served the community as a harbour, thought how much he would like to be going with Fiona to the Mainland. He was restless for new places and new people. It was a long time since he had sailed that wide, wild ocean. With a wave of nostalgia he re-membered every detail of that eventful journey to Iceland when he was a boy. Against his parents wishes he had run away to sea with a Viking sea captain called Baldur. The ship was built for heavy seas and long journeys, of oak with a pine mast forty foot high; the keel, the stem and the stern-post all of a single piece of timber; the sixteen rows of planking overlapping each other, riveted and caulked with tarred rope. The rudder was an oar of oak, eleven feet long, fastened to the starboard and mak-ing the ship very sensitive to the steersman's hand. The prow rose high and was carved like the head of a strange beast.

It rode challengingly in front, fiercely protective, the long white wake streaming back from its flanks, its eyes of red gar-net catching the glint of the sun menacingly.

When there was no wind the men rowed, singing rhythmi-cally as they did so, a deep-throated, growling song that seemed to make the boat swim faster. The slightest breeze and the striped sail was up, filling and swelling, and tugging at the boat. Neil loved it all – the keen sharp tang of the salt air; the swoop and wheel of the sea birds as they passed the islands; the sun-sparked spindrift and the heave and roll of the waves.

One evening Neil remembered he had seen a flock of small dark birds following the ship with a light bouncing flight. They darted close above the water with little fluttering wing beats, even occasionally pattering along the water with their feet as though they were running. He could almost still hear their small, twittering, urgent cries.

'Storm petrels,' Baldur had said, looking grave.

About midnight Neil had woken with a jerk as he was flung across the cabin. It felt as though he had been picked up by a giant hand and dropped from a great height. Everyone was yelling. Everyone was up and about, lurching against each other, dragging ropes, fastening things, trying to catch things that were being flung about.

One man, Othar, was crouched down in the prow of the vessel, his arms clutching the base of the beast, muttering over and over to himself the words of a Viking prayer to the Lord of the Sea. Water swamped over him but he never let go or stopped murmuring.

Wherever Neil went he heard the men praying to Odin or Thor or Aegir – never to the Lord God of Hosts, the Christian God. He propped himself between his sea chest and the wall, composed his hands and shut his eyes. He began to repeat the Lord's prayer as Brother Durston had taught him, over and over again, listening to the thunder, not thinking what he was saying. He suddenly realized what he was doing. He stopped. His words were as heathen as the others if he was not continually and deeply aware of what he was saying. His prayer had become no better than a magical chant.

A lightning flash split the sky from top to bottom. The whole ship rocked and rumbled with the shock of the thunder's sound. The beast's head was suddenly illumined by a glaring and sickening green light. It seemed to leap and whirl off the ship's prow and then the creature dissolved in yellow smoke and was no more.

Neil wondered now if Sir Kenneth sailing the same sea had felt any uneasiness about the future. Had any ill omen cast a shadow over *his* heart as the destruction of their prow guardian had cast over theirs? He tried to remember Kenneth, but could scarcely recall a single feature. He had not, at the time of his visit the year before, realized that he was to be his brother-in-law. He remembered a group of men his family had entertained from the Scottish court. He had enjoyed the ale and the dancing, and the heroic tales told by the firelight, but his attention had been caught more by a grizzled old warrior who had fought as a lad in the bloody battle that had unseated Macbeth and installed the present king's father on the throne.

Kenneth's ship was in sight now, steadily sailing with the wind behind it, growing larger every moment. At last it was near enough for the tiny figures aboard to be seen. Neil looked at Fiona and noticed that though she sat very straight, she was constantly changing Moon-Metal's reins from one hand to the other, constantly swallowing, wetting her lips, smoothing back the strands of red-gold curl that the sea wind was whipping into her face. Moon-Metal herself had caught something of her new rider's nervousness and moved uneasily from foot to foot, occasionally tossing her head and pulling against the bit.

He looked at Mairi and she was sitting still, her gaze far away. She had not even noticed the approaching sail. He remembered that she believed that 'her people' had come from the far west, from the mysterious, legendary lands beyond the setting sun. She was staring to the West now, probing the horizon with a passionate dark gaze as though she could see beyond the immeasurable watery leagues to the homeland that had once been hers.

Durston had once told him about a great sage called Pythagoras who believed that our souls could return to earth many times and inhabit many different bodies. He described the earth as a kind of academy in which we had to progress from class to class, learning all the while, until at last we were fit to leave the earth altogether and pass on to higher, unimaginable realms. Did Mairi believe this? Did she believe her soul had lived on earth before and she had been one of those ancient people who walked the avenue at Callanish? Or did she think only that they were her ancestors appearing to her now in ghost-form – faint tracings on the pages of Time? Or was it possible that in our deepest inner Self – the one we are too busy to notice, but which in our serious, quiet moments we *know* to be there – there is no Time? That in fact we are living at this moment different lives on all kinds of different levels, our progress towards wisdom influenced without our being aware of it by the rich and various events of all these different lives – a web of experience of infinite extension.

Mairi must have felt his eyes on her for she suddenly turned her head and looked at him. There was a strange expression in them and he felt a little chill down his spine. She leant towards him and he could see that she wanted to speak to him. He guided Flame closer to her.

'Neil,' she whispered. 'I am frightened. There is a shadow.'

'What do you mean?' he asked, looking round. The sky was cloudless, the sunlight unbroken.

'Over this day.'

He was about to say something more when her mare shied as though she too could sense a shadow, and almost unseated her rider. The disturbance in turn unsettled Moon-Metal who was already ill at ease to have been parted from Mairi, and she suddenly reared up. Fiona screamed.

For a brief moment there was chaos and near disaster. The little group were very close to the edge of the cliff and Fiona could very easily have been flung over the edge had Neil not acted with extraordinary presence of mind in seizing her bridle and bringing the mare to rest.

Fiona turned on Mairi in a rage.

'You nearly killed me!'

Mairi looked shocked. Was the shadow she had sensed lying in her hand to give? She shuddered, and wondered if she were after all being used by forces that were evil.

Luckily at this moment the attention of everyone on the cliff was diverted from the incident by a shout from below. The ship was drawing in close and it was time for them to start the descent of the steep path to the beach.

Fiona jerked the bit irritably in Moon-Metal's mouth, and

the mare snorted with pain. Neil touched Mairi's arm to warn her not to intervene and placed himself between the two young women on the zig-zag path.

The fishermen's coracles were drawn up well out of reach of the breakers to make space for the grand Scottish boat to anchor.

As though practising for her new role as a grand lady, Fiona imperiously arranged the small group on the shore. She herself in the front with her father and Neil behind her, slightly to one side. Behind them were the younger brothers and Mairi – and beyond these the men who had come to help transport the baggage back to the farm house.

Fiona for all her grand airs was noticeably nervous. She arranged the folds of her long skirt carefully and then rearranged them several times. She looked over her shoulder more than once as though to assure herself that her companions were still with her.

At last the ship drew near enough for her to see her future husband standing at the prow beside the Captain. Her heart gave a leap and then fell. Even from that distance she could see that he was a very handsome man . . . but he was a stranger who lived among strangers. Her courage almost failed her. She turned quickly and beckoned Mairi. The girl hesitated a moment, and Fiona repeated her gesture impatiently.

Mairi came to her side and looked at her enquiringly.

'Stay with me,' Fiona whispered. 'Do not leave me.' Her previous anger was forgotten. Mairi was back in favour.

The two young women sat side by side watching the ship's crew throw the anchor overboard and lower a little boat for the last part of the journey to the shore.

Sir Kenneth stood upright – tall, broad-shouldered, well-proportioned. As he came nearer they could see his cheerful smile and handsome face. He leapt lightly to the strand. He was just about to bow respectfully to his bride when his eye fell on the silver-white mare she rode. There was an unmistakeable expression of shocked recognition in his eyes. For a moment it seemed as though he were going to ignore Fiona altogether.

Neil could see he had momentarily forgotten her presence. Not knowing what was going on but alert as always to anything that concerned Moon-Metal and Mairi, he moved forward at once and greeted the young Mainlander loudly, half interposing Flame between his sister and her bridegroom. Sir Kenneth looked up at him, startled, and spoke some polite words in answer to his greeting. Moon-Metal trampled uneasily as she was almost pushed aside by Flame. Fiona was fully occupied getting her back under control. She was furious with Neil. What did he think he was doing – spoiling her great moment like that?

The incident however gave Sir Kenneth time to consider his reaction to the situation, and he must have decided that whatever he had been about to say could wait, for he took his eyes off the white mare and directed them to Fiona, greeting her with a grave and formal politeness that belied the warmth of the feelings he had once expressed so passionately.

Happily unaware of any uneasy undercurrents, Fiona's father made his speech of welcome. His men were deputed to dismount and deliver their horses to Sir Kenneth and his two friends, Sir Roger and Sir Geoffrey, and to offer their services to the young lord's men in unloading the ship. Fiona, thoroughly put out by the fact that she was not the centre of attention as she had expected to be, sulkily hung back and allowed her father to lead the party up the cliff path.

Neil made it his business to stay as close as he could to Sir Kenneth and, when the path broadened out at the top of the cliff, he rode beside him.

'What kind of a voyage did you have, sir?' he asked, wondering how he could broach the subject of the white mare.

'All I can say about the voyage,' the young man replied with feeling, 'is that I'm glad it is over.'

Neil laughed. 'We had a fierce storm here a day or two ago. I know what such storms can be like at sea!'

'We had our share of storms. Indeed we would have been here sooner had we not.'

Neil could tell that Sir Kenneth's attention was only half on what he was saying and he decided to ask him outright what was troubling him. But at that moment the attention of both of them was distracted by a rider breasting the hill from the direction of the farm house. It was Donal.

As soon as he was near enough for the sword at his side to be seen, Sir Kenneth gave a fierce shout and he and his two companions broke from the others, drove their heels into their steeds and rode fast to meet him.

In amazement Neil, Fiona, Lorn and Mairi saw Kenneth gallop up to Donal, his sword drawn, while his two friends took up positions obviously intended to prevent Donal escaping.

Donal, astonished, reined in his horse and clumsily drew out his own sword.

The others were too far away to hear or see exactly what was happening, but it was clear that Donal was being challenged and threatened. Sensing some excitement, the dogs raced up to the small group, circling and barking.

Donal was totally confused. He had returned home after his adventures to find that his sister had miraculously recovered from her paralysis, and that the girl he had been sent to find and who had been accused of being a witch was an honoured visitor at his home. Now the young man who was to be his brother-in-law and whom he had been sent out so precipitously to greet, was shouting insults and threatening him with a deadly looking weapon.

As far as he knew everything had turned around here too and Sir Kenneth was proving to be an enemy and not a friend to his family.

He lunged at him vigorously with his new-found sword. This seemed to madden the Mainlanders even more and all three circled him with weapons drawn.

Having recovered from the initial shock of surprise and seeing that Donal was in danger, Neil rode forward, shouting for calm. His shouts were misinterpreted and Kenneth's friends rounded on him, leaving Kenneth to deal with Donal alone. This brought Lorn forward angrily and for a while there was a melee of horses and weapons and angry men – none in fact actually drawing blood – but all on the verge of it.

Fiona and Mairi were horrified. How could this be happening? One moment there was pleasant and polite conversation between civilized people, and the next there was violence and hostility.

With scarcely any effort on the part of the Mainlanders, the surprised Islanders were unseated from their horses and herded, unarmed, into a tight group – Sir Kenneth holding the point of his sword at Donal's throat.

'Now speak,' he said fiercely. 'Where did you get that sword, that dagger and . . .' he jerked his head in the direction of Moon-Metal . . . 'that white mare?'

Donal gaped at him.

'Speak!' commanded Sir Kenneth, driving his sword tip a fraction nearer to Donal's fragile windpipe.

'I . . . I found the weapons . . .'

'Found? Where?'

'Lying in the heather.'

'You lie!'

At this moment Fiona and Mairi rode up.

'How dare you!' Fiona said haughtily. 'Put down that sword at once!'

Neil had often thought that an avenging angel must look much like Fiona when she was angry – very, very beautiful and very, very fierce. Sir Kenneth looked into her fiery green eyes and lowered his sword.

'Explain yourself!' she commanded.

'It is I who need an explanation,' Sir Kenneth said coldly.

'You have attacked one of my brothers for no reason, and humiliated my father and my other brother. It is *I*, sir, who am owed an explanation.'

'The weapons your brother wears, my lady, and the mare you ride, belong to my brother. He disappeared without trace and my family believe he was robbed and murdered.'

Shocked – Fiona and Neil looked at Mairi. Donal went white. How he regretted that he had not taken the trouble to give the dead man Christian burial, but had just taken his weapons and ridden on. Brother Durston had told him once when he was a child that there was no way of escaping the consequences of one's actions no matter how secretly they were performed.

'You are wrong, sir,' Mairi spoke up suddenly. 'The mare is mine. It was given to me as a gift. But of the weapons I know nothing.'

'Who gave you the mare?'

She hesitated – not knowing how to explain what she believed to be the truth – even beginning herself to doubt what she believed had happened.

'My brother would never have given his horse or his weapons away,' Sir Kenneth said icily. 'They were his most treasured possessions.'

'Are you accusing my family of being thieves and liars – possibly even murderers?' Lorn spoke up at last. 'If this is what you think of us, sir, you will not be surprised if I withdraw my permission for you to marry my daughter.'

On the ship Sir Kenneth had questioned his commitment to the marriage, but now the fiery, tempestuous woman before him stirred his blood. She was more, much more than the lively, pretty girl he remembered. Her beauty and her strength of spirit would be a great help to him in the changeable, challenging world of the Mainland.

'It seems I have wronged your family, sir,' he began, 'but . . .'

'Of course you have wronged my family,' interrupted Fiona fiercely.

'I apologise for being so quick to draw my sword,' he said. 'But these are bad times and I have been taught to trust no one.' He paused and looked pointedly at Donal. 'Perhaps you have news of my brother?'

'Believe me,' Donal said hastily. 'I had no idea that these weapons belonged to your brother and would never have taken them if I had known. I found them in the heather – abandoned. The mare is a different matter. For an explanation of that you will have to ask . . .' And here he looked at Mairi darkly.

'My mother is waiting with a welcome feast prepared,' Neil interrupted hastily. 'It is clear, Sir Kenneth, no deliberate villainy has occurred. We, as urgently as you, need to get to the bottom of this mystery.'

He managed to get the little party somehow to follow him to the house, an uneasy truce wordlessly declared.

Neil looked at Mairi and could see that her face was very troubled.

At the sound of approaching horses Ingrid rushed out to greet them, the smile fading from her eyes when she saw how morose and gloomy they all looked.

Sir Kenneth responded to her greeting politely, and introduced his two friends who bowed without smiling. She looked enquiringly at her husband but all he did was turn away to give instructions to his men about the horses and baggage. Puzzled, but not daunted, she bustled them into the hall, where she clapped her hands for their cloaks to be taken and refreshment to be brought. She chattered on as though nothing was amiss. Had Sir Kenneth changed his mind about the marriage? She could not believe it. Fiona had never looked more beautiful and any man would be honoured by taking such a wife. She looked at Mairi seated on Fiona's left hand. Her head was drooping, her cheeks pale, and there was a look of absolute desolation in every line of her body. If anything had gone wrong it must have something to do with 'that girl'!

Donal, following his mother's gaze, had a flash of inspiration. 'Sir Kenneth,' he said. 'I am sure we will find the key to our mystery has something to do with witchcraft.' He made a point of looking at Mairi so hard it was impossible to miss the implication.

Kenneth looked at Mairi.

'What is this, lady?' he demanded sharply.

At this point if Mairi had replied only that she had found the mare wandering riderless, as indeed she had, she would have been saved a great deal of suffering. But she was so convinced of the reality of 'her people' and their gift to her of this magical mare when she needed it, that she insisted on telling Sir Kenneth about the Tall Stones and the ancient priests who spoke to her. Neil tried to interrupt and divert her but, cheeks flushed, eyes bright, she pressed on, sure that everything would be all right if she just told the truth.

It was only when she had finished the tale that she noticed that the room had grown silent and everywhere she looked she was met by a dark and implacable stare of misunderstanding. Bewildered she looked at Neil. In his eyes at least there was pity . . . but also dismay.

Donal leapt up.

'I have been to this girl's village,' he cried. 'I have heard her own father denounce her as a witch. She goes regularly to those Devil's Stones she talks so glibly about and meets with evil spirits. It is clear that they must have sacrificed your brother in their fiendish ceremonies and given her his horse for her part in them.'

'No!' cried Mairi, her face ashen.

'Yes!' shouted Donal.

'Yes!' shouted dozens of voices.

The hall was in an uproar, people stamping and shouting, faces angry, fists raised. Sir Kenneth stared at Mairi in horror. To him she looked like a witch. White face . . . sloe black hair . . . and an extraordinary, almost unearthly beauty.

Neil put his left arm around her fiercely, and gripped his knife with his right hand ready to defend her to the death if necessary.

'She is no witch. I swear it!' he shouted. 'Believe me . . .'

'She is condemned by her own mouth!' yelled Donal.

'She has put a spell on you as she put a spell on me!' called out Fiona, so carried away by the violent emotions in the crowd that she once again forgot the truth of her recent experience.

Suddenly the tall figure of the hermit emerged from the shadows near the door and strode into the centre of the room. He stood behind Mairi, towering above her. He raised his hand for silence, his dark eyes compelling attention as he stared the ringleaders down one by one. When there was silence at last, he continued to stand, like the deep shadow of a rock at night, his arm raised, his hand over them. Those who had been quickest to accuse were the first to want to drop their eyes, but found that they could not. At last, when the waiting had become almost intolerable, he spoke.

'There is a dark spirit in this room now and it is not in the body of this girl. It is in the mind of you and you and you . . .' he pointed his finger first at Donal and then at everyone who had leapt so quickly to the condemnation of Mairi. 'What will you do? Tear her apart? Is that what Christ would have done? Is it?' His eyes were blazing.

No one answered. There was an awkward silence and a restless shifting about on the benches and the stools. Some felt guilty, some resentful, but none felt like answering his challenge.

It was Sir Kenneth who at last had the courage to speak out.

'But if it is true . . .' he began.

'If it is true . . . even if it is true . . . would Christ condone what is in your hearts at this time?' Brother Durston's hawk eyes fixed on his.

'But Christ is not here,' muttered someone.

Durston turned his face to the speaker and the man cringed. 'Does anyone else think that Christ is not here?' he asked in an awesome voice. No one spoke. Neil could feel Mairi trembling under his arm like a trapped bird. She had turned her face into his shoulder as she had done before.

It was Sir Kenneth who again broke the painful silence. 'Whether the girl is in league with the devil or not I do not know. Those who have known her longer must be the judge of that. But what I do know is that she had my brother's mare and until I have a satisfactory explanation of that I will not be content.'

Neil spoke up suddenly. 'Donal accuses her of fiendish practices. What proof does he have? As I see it, she found the mare wandering riderless, deserted. Your brother most probably met with an accident – or maybe he was set upon by thieves.'

Mairi freed her head from his restraining hand and looked up as though she was about to deny his explanation, which she thought threw doubt on the existence of 'her people'.

'Hush,' he whispered. 'Say nothing.'

She obeyed but drew away from him – her shoulder turned to him and her eyes cast down – her hands clasping and unclasping in her lap.

Sir Kenneth was prepared to listen – but was not convinced.

'Would thieves have left my brother's mare, my brother's sword and dagger?'

Donal's mouth felt dry. He swallowed several times and wet his lips with his tongue. How he wished he had told the truth in the first place. Now with every passing moment it became more and more difficult to do so.

'I swear I found them,' he muttered.

'Where?' Kenneth demanded.

'Near . . . the Devil's Stones,' he replied.

'Is that not proof?' someone called out. 'The man was sacrificed?'

Angry murmuring against Mairi started up again.

'Not necessarily,' Donal said hastily, beginning to regret the danger in which he had placed the young woman. 'If your brother had fallen off his horse . . .'

'Then his body would have been with his weapons,' Kenneth said coldly.

'The thieves might have been frightened off by something and dropped the weapons a distance away from where they slew him.' Donal continued desperately.

It was Lorn, always the peacemaker, who rose from his place now.

'Friends,' he said mildly. 'It seems to me we can solve nothing here, in this way. I propose that in the morning Sir Kenneth and my sons ride to Callanish, enquire of people, search the area, try and trace Sir Kenneth's brother.'

'But the wedding?' wailed Fiona's mother. 'Tomorrow is Fiona's wedding day.'

Sir Kenneth looked at her gravely. 'I am afraid until this shadow is removed, madam, it is not in my heart to be married.'

Fiona bit her lip. Then she rose from her place and swept out of the hall without a backward glance.

Chapter 13

The Brother

In the morning, very early, a group gathered in the forecourt and mounted up ready to ride. Sir Kenneth and his two companions were there. Also Donal and Neil, Mairi on Moon-Metal and Brother Durston beside her on a rather sinewy, ragged looking pony belonging to one of Neil's younger brothers. He looked too large for the animal – his legs, without stirrups, dangling awkwardly near to the ground. The dogs were barking with excitement, begging to be allowed to go with the riders. Ingrid was fussing with pouches and baskets of food. Neil's father was giving instructions about care and caution. The younger brothers were running in and out, getting in the way.

Just as Donal was about to duck his head to lead them under the lintel of the gateway and out of the yard, Fiona came storming out of the house.

'Why did no one wake me?' she demanded. She was dressed in her usual brown homespun, her summer cape flung over her shoulders, her hair unbound. There was no sign of the elegant young lady in silk brocade pretending to be a Mainlander. She appeared, as she was, a sturdy young woman of the Western Isles, the sharp air of early dawn fairly crackling around her as she moved.

'But you are not going Fiona!' cried her mother.

'Of course I am going,' Fiona declared impatiently. 'Why should I not go?'

She snapped her fingers for someone to bring her a horse. Mairi at once started to slide off the back of the white mare.

'No,' Fiona said. 'I will not touch her again until we know the truth.'

The 'truth'? Neil thought. And how would they ever know that? But he said nothing.

Sir Kenneth dismounted and solicitously tried to help her onto the horse that had been brought forward for her. She shrugged away his hand and mounted swiftly and easily by herself.

His two friends looked at each other, amused, wondering what kind of life Kenneth would have with such a firebrand. She was already under the lintel and off, leading the party without a backward glance.

Lorn put his hand on his wife's arm to restrain her from rushing after her to bring her back.

'Let her go,' he said quietly. 'It is right that she goes.' He was glad Brother Durston, who never went anywhere, had made an exception this time. 'They will be all right,' he added with confidence. And then, as the sound of hooves faded, he turned his attention back with relief to the animals he understood and the calm and ancient earth.

Rain in the night had washed everything clear and clean. The tide was far out as the group of riders reached the sands and, pure and dazzling, the huge expanse of powdered white crystal lay without a mark as though it had just been created. Neil wished there was some way to reach back to the beginning of the world to start again. As far back as he knew there had been invasions, hatred, killing. The Vikings had not begun it. There were other invaders, other battles, other conquerors – the victors of one century, the victims of the next. The Christ had come to earth to break the vicious circle of violence and exploitation, yet just a few years before an army of Christians had mustered to invade the Holy Land and take it by force, killing all who opposed them. What for? It was an empty shell. As Brother Durston said: Christ is here. Wherever man is, Christ is. Thou shalt not kill. Thou shalt love thy God and thy neighbour. Thou shalt forgive as thou would'st be forgiven.

He had once seen a small bird trapped in a room, hovering

before a mirror and pecking at its own reflection in a frenzy, believing it to be an enemy.

Just before they passed between the high rock walls of Glen Valtos the group dismounted and rested a while. The storm waters had subsided and the whole place seemed very different to Neil from the last time he had passed that way.

Fiona sat on a large boulder almost in the centre of the stream, throwing small pebbles into the water. Kenneth stood on the bank, watching her. Mairi stayed close beside Moon- metal, stroking her flank as the mare drank from the river, talking softly to her. Brother Durston sat some way away from the others, his eyes shut, his face lifted up to the sky; still alone, a hermit though surrounded by people.

Neil looked around for the others. Donal was with Kenneth's two companions, boasting about his prowess as a wrestler and the women who had admired him for it. He heard their laughter as his brother told one anecdote after another.

He was suddenly impatient to move on, impatient to get things understood and settled, impatient to know the truth. He whistled to Flame and sprang onto his back. It was not long before the others joined him and they were deep into the gorge.

As they passed the ledge where he and Mairi had spent the night of the storm he looked back at her to see if she remembered. She had and, for the first time since Donal had accused her in his parent's hall, a smile flickered across her face as she met his eyes. He slowed Flame's pace until he was level with Moon-Metal.

'You mustn't worry,' he said. 'Everything changes. We would not have believed the last time we were here that the river could be as gentle as it is today.'

Donal and Kenneth's two friends were now riding ahead – recklessly setting a pace too fast to be prudent in the narrow glen. The sound of their hooves pounding and their voices shouting echoed back and forth among the rocks and caused Kenneth to look with some trepidation at the great boulders almost cut through by frost and poised, ready to fall. He would not like to be caught in such a place if there were a rock fall. He thought about his brother. He had stayed on the island when Kenneth left for the mainland. They had heard from him from time to time, but not for over a year now. When Kenneth was on the island the year before, he had intended to see his brother but had been distracted by meeting Fiona, and had returned home without making contact. It was only a couple of months ago that a friend of his brother's had brought news that no one had seen him for such a long time they wondered if he were dead. The Western Isles were settled since the firm rule of Magnus Barefoot, yet violence and disorder were never far from the surface, some Islanders resenting Norse rule. Disaffected sons of dispossessed families, escaped slaves, ordinary criminals, drifted from place to place and preyed on others. It was also known that quite a few native Gaels from the Mainland had taken shelter on the Islands to escape the hated English and Norman influence begun at the time of Malcolm and Margaret. With no kin and no land many of them lived as outlaws.

Riding now through the gloomy glen, Kenneth stared at Mairi riding ahead on his brother's white mare and swore that if she was responsible for any harm having come to his brother, she would cry out for death to release her from his vengeance.

At this moment she looked back over her shoulder at him and her face was filled with fear. It was as though she had heard his thoughts! 'My God!' Kenneth thought. 'She *is* in league with the Devil!' He did not remember the many times he himself had looked up in response to the pressure of someone else's thought.

'That bitch shall not ride her!' he suddenly shouted and rode angrily forward. Neil looked back in time to see him seize Mairi and haul her off the back of the mare.

He was instantly at her side, driving Flame between them.

'What is the matter with you?' he shouted. 'Hold back! Hold back I say!' It looked almost as though Kenneth intended to strike her.

Neil stooped down and picked Mairi up, placing her in front

of him on Flame. With eyes flashing angrily but without a word, he rode forward until he was well ahead of Kenneth and the rest. Mairi clung desperately to him, shaking almost uncontrollably.

They skirted the long sea inlet of Little Loch Roag and then had a decision to make. They could make camp and rest, arriving at Callanish fresh in the morning. Or they could continue as quickly as possible and arrive well into the evening – exhausted.

In spite of Brother Durston's persuasive plea for the former, they decided to opt for the latter.

As they approached the area in which the dead man lay, Donal became more and more uneasy. He had passed the time exchanging tall tales with Sir Roger and Sir Geoffrey about their respective prowess with women and in battle and had not properly considered the problem as to whether he would lead Sir Kenneth to his brother or not before the heather clad headland of Callanish actually came in sight. He told himself that there had been no harm done in leaving the man where he had found him. After all, he had been there a long while. If only he had not taken the weapons or – if he had not lied about them. He wrestled with his conscience a hundred different ways and he found the match more difficult than any he had fought with others. If the man was Kenneth's brother, and it was clear that he was, it was only right that Kenneth should be given a chance to pay his respects to his kin and to see him decently buried with prayers for the safe conduct of his soul. To die so suddenly, unshriven of sins committed, would surely mean the man's soul was wandering haplessly in limbo. A priest could lift that soul to God. And yet, if Donal showed that he knew where the man lay it would become clear that he had taken the weapons as any un-Christian robber would have done, leaving the man's soul unaided. He began to imagine him wandering in a grey and featureless place, desperately calling for help while Donal shut his ears and walked away.

He looked at Brother Durston, incongruously large on a small Island horse, and wished that he had the courage to confess to him. But the shame of what he had tried to do to Mairi in order to save his own face, and fear of the stern, searching gaze of the hermit's eyes was too much for him.

He rode up to Neil and Mairi.

'I . . . saw your parents,' he said to Mairi. His voice much humbler than it had been in the hall the night before.

Mairi looked up at him over Neil's shoulder.

'So you said before,' Neil said coldly. He was still angry with his brother and no matter which way he looked at his cruelty to Mairi he could not find a way to forgive him.

'Your father . . .' Donal persisted, determined at least to try to soften things for the girl. 'Your father said the things I told you about last night, but . . .' he winced slightly at the fierce glare he received from Neil. 'But your mother denied everything he said. She loves you and believes in you . . . and wanted me to tell you that.'

'It is a pity you did not say that last night,' snapped Neil.

'He has said it now,' said Durston quietly moving up on the left side of Mairi and Neil.

'It is too late.'

'It is never too late to repent,' said Durston drily.

Mairi looked gratefully at Donal. 'Thank you,' she said. 'Is my mother all right?'

Donal could tell by her voice that she knew very well how things were between her mother and her father and that it was more than likely that she was not at all all right.

He did not want to add to her pain again. 'She is all right,' he said. 'She loves you.'

Mairi looked sadly over the hills towards her mother's house. Skena had never understood her daughter, but at least she had never condemned her. Mairi thought back to her mother's own mother who had died when she had seen the angel: an old, old woman of great wisdom. Mairi and she had never spoken about the people of the crystal Eye because Mairi had not yet met them when she was still alive, but the girl believed that she would have understood about them, and sometimes she wondered if she might not have seen them herself. She often talked about the great tree spirits that were close to God, yet not high in the sky nor deep in the earth.

'Time and Space are for children,' her grandmother used to say, forgetting that she was talking to a child. 'Angels exist in a way it is impossible for us to imagine – without Time or Space.'

'Do they hear us if we call to them?' Mairi had asked.

'They have no ears. They cannot hear words.'

'If we want to call on their help – how do we do it?'

'We feel it in our heart. We yearn for it in our soul.'

'Sometimes I have done that and they have not come.'

'Perhaps they have – but you have not recognised them.'

Suddenly one of the dogs who had followed them all the way from Uig broke away from them – following a hare that was leaping and bouncing off the heather. The other dogs instantly set up a tremendous show of barking and went running after him. Kenneth's two friends, bored with the last few miles of silence from Donal and what to them was a featureless landscape after the tree-clad mountains of their home country, enthusiastically set off in pursuit.

The hare must have disappeared down a hole for the dogs suddenly stopped running and crowded round a particular place, barking and wagging their tails excitedly. The two men on horseback galloped up behind the dogs, and the others saw one of them dismount.

Donal felt sick. He knew that they would not find a hare in that hole, but Kenneth's brother. Was every deed noted in heaven as the priest said? Nothing hidden that would not be revealed? He began to sweat.

Sir Roger galloped back towards them, while the dogs and Sir Geoffrey stayed beside the place. It was as though Donal could see the words forming in the mind of the man before his voice shouted them out to Kenneth.

Within seconds they were all riding across the rough terrain and crowding round the hole the dogs had found.

Donal stood behind Kenneth and looked over his shoulder as Geoffrey moved the bushes back, into the eye-sockets of the man he had left in limbo.

The Standing Stones of Callanish and all their secrets were temporarily forgotten as, in the fading light of late evening, they struggled to get the body up from the deep cleft. There had been a rock fall, and the man was heavily pinned down.

The sky over the great sea loch was scarlet and vermilion when they at last succeeded in bringing him to the surface. Kenneth stood looking down at him silently as his friends laid him on the dark heather. Then he stooped and covered him with his cloak. There were tears in his eyes.

Quietly Fiona moved forward and took his hand.

Behind him and at a little distance, Mairi stood with her hand in Neil's hand.

Donal stood awkwardly nearby, the dogs panting beside him, their tongues lolling, unaware of what they had done.

After a while Kenneth seemed to pull himself together. Donal could see him squaring his shoulders and taking a deep breath. His heart sank. Now would come the reckoning.

Kenneth turned and looked at the man who had so boldly worn his brother's weapons, and then he strode towards him. Donal clenched his fists nervously, wishing for the first time in his life that he could turn and run from another man. He had no stomach for this fight.

Kenneth stood in front of him and his face was stern and cold.

'You killed him,' he said and his voice was harsh and bitter.

'No!' gasped Donal. 'I swear it. No. I . . . I found him . . .'

'Found him?'

'In the hole . . . I mean . . . he was already dead a long time . . . I fell into it myself. That . . . that is how I found him. His horse must have . . .'

The little group had gathered round him. Now he knew how

Mairi must have felt. He had never thought that people would look at *him* like that. Sir Roger and Sir Geoffrey with whom he had been joking all the way from Uig had drawn their swords . . . their faces were the faces of strangers.

'You found a man lying in a ditch and you did not bring him to the church for Christian burial?' Sir Kenneth said, his voice like ice.

Donal flushed. 'I . . . I was in a hurry . . . I meant to go back . . . but . . .'

'Why did you not tell me this when I first challenged you about the weapons? Why did you lie and lie and LIE!' his voice was rising with every word. 'Why did you not lead me straight to my brother? What would you have done if the dogs had not found him?' His face was distorted with rage. He pulled out his dagger and leapt at Donal. 'Whether you killed his body or left it to rot unshriven is all one to me. You die!' he shouted and raised his arm. Horrified Donal seized his wrist and used all his strength to turn the blade. He fought with all his strength, the two men straining every muscle against each other, blind to their lives stretching before or after – throwing all on this one fierce moment.

Kenneth's two companions stood back and let them fight, their eyes gleaming with excitement. Neil put his restraining arms around Fiona who was screaming and crying and trying to part them. The dogs were barking, the horses backing and whinnying with alarm. Durston and Mairi stood close together, watching.

'Stop them!' screamed Fiona to Durston. 'Why do you let them kill each other!' Tears were streaming down her cheeks and she was now beating at Neil in a desperate attempt to free herself. The dagger had been flung aside by Donal and the two men were now rolling over and over on the ground, the heather crackling under their weight.

'Kenneth! Donal!' shrieked Fiona frantically. 'Stop them!' she cried again to Durston.

'And if I stop them – will that stop the anger in the heart of one and the guilt in the heart of the other?'

Fiona's furious exclamation was lost as Neil clapped his hand over his sister's mouth.

But in spite of his words Durston moved forward.

'Stop!' he roared in a voice of thunder. 'In God's name stop, I say! God is the one and only true judge.'

He had chosen the moment well. Startled – they looked up.

The setting sun was causing a vast and flaring aura of fire and light around him and he seemed at that moment like one of the great archangels.

They drew apart – bruised and bloodstained.

They stood up and dusted themselves off, breathless, unable to speak.

Fiona looked from one to the other, weeping. Who should she condemn; who defend? She loved them both.

Mairi came forward and slipped her hand quietly into hers.

* * * *

As they approached Kirkoway Neil could feel Mairi trembling and tightened his arm around her.

'It will be all right,' he whispered into her hair. 'I won't let them touch you.'

'How will I stop them?' he thought. 'Why do I say it will be all right when I have no idea if it will be?'

But he continued murmuring to her as he would to a nervous animal, hoping the sound of his voice and the warmth of his body against hers would comfort her.

Someone in the village must have spotted them, for it seemed the whole male population of Kirkoway was gathered blocking the road into the village. Every man and boy was armed with pitch-fork or axe or stone. The face of every man and boy was set hard and unwelcoming. Braden, in the forefront, held a large wooden cross out in front of him with his left hand while gripping an axe with his right.

The villagers had first seen a line of lights snaking over the hills from the direction of the Devil's Stones and had instantly assumed they were to be visited by demons, roused by a vengeful Mairi. Braden had lost no time in spreading the rumour that she had cursed a young woman at Uig who was now paralysed.

Sir Kenneth reined in sharp, surprised by the belligerence of the welcome. His companions bunched up around him, only Neil and Mairi standing off behind, away from the torchlight, hoping to pass unnoticed. Durston moved up beside Kenneth, slipping to the ground.

'What is this?' demanded Kenneth coldly. 'Is this the way Christians welcome weary travellers?'

'Do you travel in the name of Christ?'

Before Kenneth could answer Durston stepped forward in his monk's habit.

'We do, brother,' he said in his deep and resonating voice. 'Do you?'

Braden looked at him discomforted. Sir Kenneth and the two men on either side of him were plainly no raggle-taggle demons, but handsome and well clad members of the nobility – by their style – probably from the Mainland. And here with them was a priest.

Braden lowered his cross and his axe, the other villagers following his lead.

'Forgive us Brother,' Braden said gruffly, 'but we were expecting demons.'

Durston threw back his head and laughed.

'Demons don't come when you expect them, brother,' he said, 'nor from God's hills and valleys. You have to look into your own heart for demons,' he added, more seriously, 'and there no axe will defeat them.'

Braden was clearly offended by Durston's laughter and his face darkened. He handed the cross to his neighbour and took over his torch. He held it so that he could see the monk more closely. On his chest, instead of the crucifix, hung the silver outline of a fish. Durston saw him looking at it with incomprehension and decided to set his mind at ease by unfastening the rosary from the cord at his waist and holding it out so that the light of the torch flickered on the crystal beads and the little cross of driftwood.

'Have you not heard that the Christ was the fisher of men?' he asked mildly.

Braden bit his lip. He had taken an instant dislike to the hermit – but a monk's habit – and a rosary – and three noblemen – how could he turn them away?

But at that moment his eye fell on Mairi and he let out a roar of anger and brandished his axe again.

'You wear the Lord's raiment,' he shouted, 'but you are in the company of the Devil's child!'

Sir Kenneth had had enough.

'We are no followers of demons, man, we are friends of Jarl Erickson and have come to seek Christian burial for my brother. Do we turn aside and find another village, another church to give us welcome? Do we tell the Jarl that Kirkoway gave us no place to rest, no bread, no prayers for our dead?'

Other villagers moved forward now and pushed Braden aside. Jarl Erikson was a powerful man – well known and well respected on the Island.

'Go no further, sir. You are welcome in our village. Forgive our caution but . . .' And then they too spotted Mairi and hesitated.

'This is a young woman of your own village I believe,' Kenneth said. 'We know nothing of her except that she has been kind enough to lead us here.'

'She'll put no foot in this village,' snarled Braden.

Fiona and Donal rode forward now.

'Sir,' said Donal. 'This is my sister. I was mistaken when I told you she had been cursed and paralysed. As you can see – there is nothing the matter with her.'

Suddenly Neil lowered Mairi to the ground and rode up close to Braden. From his height on Flame's back he glared down at the man.

'Mairi is no witch-child, no devil-consort, and well you know it! Neither is the white mare a demon-steed. It belonged to a Mainland lord, this knight's brother, who met with an accident. Mairi found the mare wandering and lost without a master, and took it home as any of us might have done.'

At this moment the women who had been watching from the shadows came rushing forward to welcome the strangers in. So many handsome men! Such elegance! Such rich apparel!

Skena rushed straight to Mairi and mother and daughter fell into each other's arms.

Braden was pushed aside, and though no one actually spoke to Mairi – indeed they gave her a wide berth – no one prevented her entering the village with her mother.

The body of Sir Kenneth's brother was taken to the little stone church on the hill overlooking the loch and reverently laid, wrapped in Sir Kenneth's cloak, before the altar. The itinerant priest who would normally officiate at a funeral was not in Kirkoway at the moment, so Brother Durston knelt and prayed beside him.

Sir Kenneth and Donal also remained in the church with him – on their knees – in vigil all night.

The burial would be in the morning.

As for the rest of the party from Uig – they were taken in by the villagers and given shelter. Fiona and Neil insisted on staying with Mairi – the two young women in one bed – Neil on the floor.

Candlelight fell on the cloak that hid the sorry heap of discarded bones that had once been a vigorous young man. Kenneth's anger had passed and beneath it the pain was now naked and exposed. Memories came crowding back. Memories of being a child on the Island with his brother as his constant companion – racing along the beaches, fencing with wooden swords, testing each other out in every way familiar to young boys – wrestling, running, jumping . . .

Always vying for attention. Those early years had seemed as though they would last forever. The brothers were inseparable. Their love for each other unclouded.

But then had come the separation. At one stage Ian sought adventure in the Crusades, while Kenneth stayed in Scotland and enjoyed a gentler, more secure life. Surely this ignominious end had not come to Ian? He was a tough soldier who had defended himself against Saracen hordes. How could he have met his death, so young, on this relatively peaceful island?

Kenneth shivered. On what a delicate thread our lives hang? Kenneth knew all about death of course – but never had he felt its shadow so keenly. 'Strange,' he thought, 'it is the one thing, the only thing, certain in life, and yet it is always a surprise, always a shock.'

He stared at the silence that had been his brother. He stared at the gaping hole where there had once been laughter and shouting and racing and loving.

Where was he now, his brother? If the scriptures and the priests were right he would either be in heaven or hell. Unimaginable places. He thought about the descriptions of both he had heard and could believe neither. The very fact of his having been on the crusades should have earned him a place in heaven. But Christ had said: 'Judge not, that ye be not judged. For with what judgement ye judge, ye shall be judged: and with what measure ye mete, it shall be measured to you again. And why beholdest thou the mote that is in thy brother's eye, but considerest not the beam that is in thine own eye?. . .'* How much easier it had been to ride out with drums drumming and trumpets blaring, among men accoutred in the finest armour – to kill flesh and blood enemies, than it would have been to stay home and eradicate the enemy in one's own secret heart. Because Ian had not loved his enemies as Christ had said he should – would he now be in hell? Kenneth shuddered as horrifying pictures of torture came before his eyes. But they were all pictures of the tortures men inflicted on each other on this earth. The mighty Three-in-One God was different! Had to be different if He had created all that existed. He would not stoop to such petty cruelties. No. Those pictures in the churches had to be wrong. Ian had not taken his body into the other-world to be tortured as a body could be on earth. If there was anything left of him at all – it was of a very, very different nature.

Kenneth looked down at his own body. It was familiar. He loved it. He did not want to be parted from it. He would give anything to take his brother in his arms again and feel the pressure of his warm flesh responding to his embrace. He did not want to be some disembodied spirit, some alien being, something that could not feel and hear and see . . .

Durston looked up from where he knelt and saw the suffering and the conflict in the young man's face. With his eyes still on him he prayed for him to accept the difference between this world and the next and not fear it. 'Did you not fear going to the Mainland when you were young? Have you not always feared the unknown? Yet when it is no longer the unknown you have no longer feared it?'

Kenneth began to feel calmer. If the world he could see around him was so varied and magnificent, so complex and surprising that he knew and understood so little of it in spite of all the years he had lived on it – who was he to demand that what he had not yet understood or experienced should conform to some picture he dreamed up in his blindness and his ignorance.

Durston saw that his eyes were closing and his head was drooping on his chest. Quietly he stood up, crossed the chapel and helped the man to lie down before he fell down.

Donal meanwhile was already snoring.

Chapter 14

The Eye is Closed

As though to a signal Neil jerked awake. At first he could see no reason for his waking. One moment he was deeply asleep and the next every faculty was alert. The stale darkness of the cottage was oppressive. He lifted his head and scanned the room. He heard no sound, saw no movement, yet he was convinced that something had changed.

He remembered the last time he had slept in this room and how he had woken in the small hours to follow Mairi across the moors to Callanish. He sat up quickly and looked across to the wooden bed where the two young women lay. It was extremely difficult to make out any forms in the dim light from the smouldering peat, but he could just see the shape of a figure lying on the bed. It was possible that there were two figures but he could not be sure. Being now fully awake he decided to go outside and at least breathe some fresh air for a while. Carefully he crept out of the house, trying to remember where every obstacle lay.

Once outside he was astonished how light and vibrant the night was. A huge, full, silver moon hung above him and to every horizon magnificent stars blazed out. He knew that he could not go back into that wretched cottage again. The houses of the village seemed to lend the landscape darkness.

He decided that he wanted to go to the great stone circle at Callanish. He wanted to experience for himself what Mairi had described; to test with his own faculties whether there was anything supernatural there or not.

A low whistle detached his horse from the others and he

slipped onto its back without a saddle as he had done that beautiful, golden day that now seemed so long ago – the day he and Mairi had galloped along the white crystal sands of her favourite strand – wild and free and happy.

Moon-Metal was not in the paddock with the other horses, but Neil could not be sure that Kenneth had not tethered her elsewhere. He hoped that Mairi would not be at the Stones. He wanted to be there alone . . .

But Mairi was at the Stones. Fiona had gone to sleep almost immediately, and Mairi had lain very still for a long time beside her, trying not to disturb her. If it was true that the white mare had not been given her as a gift by 'her people', but had just strayed by sheer chance to the Stones, how much more of what had happened to her would prove to have another explanation? She knew that she had been accepted back into the village because they now regarded her as a liar rather than as a witch. They seemed to have pushed the other incidents that had frightened them in the past to the back of their minds: the prophecies, the angel by the altar, the reading of people's minds, the healings . . . Was all of it illusion? Was there nothing else to life but what the others saw, the others heard and touched? Are we born, do we eat, sleep, procreate and die, and then go to a heaven or a hell not much different from this world – and that is all? Was God satisfied if you pronounced His name at frequent intervals whether you really believed in Him or not – really loved Him or not – really did His bidding or not? She would find it difficult to love such a God. It seemed to her most people had settled for a form of words and did not want to think beyond it. But she wanted to encounter her God round every corner. She wanted her perception of Him to be a continual surprise – each day a fresh discovery – a fresh reverence.

She rose and crept out of the dark house, and, as she rode over the silver-dark hills probably for the last time on Moon-Metal, she felt icily alone. She had never felt so alone – not even when her father was beating her – for then at least she had known that she had her secret people to turn to when the beating was over. If they did not exist then she did not know how she could go on living; the purpose she had held to for so long would have been taken from her and nothing put in its place. To go with Fiona to Prince David's court and be a fine lady was to her a waste of precious time, a mockery of what life was about. What would she learn there but fine words to flatter with; and what would her life be except 'passing the time' until death?

Around her she saw the heather-covered land empty and waste in a way she had never seen it before. The sheets of water that lay beneath the moon in mere and loch, seemed to her like the eyes of blind men, reflecting, but seeing nothing.

The Stones loomed at last. She climbed off the mare before she reached them and stood for a long while, hesitating before she entered the processional way. She feared to take the first step in case she found nothing there but the cold clear night and the tall slabs of stone.

But she knew she had to try. She had to know.

She took the first step. There was nothing different. Her heart almost breaking, she took another step and another. That part of her she knew to be eternal was crying to the Great Spirit for help and guidance. That part of her she knew to be temporary was doubting, despairing.

Step after step she took, at first faltering, but becoming steadier . . . slow and measured she walked forward, her back stretching to become straight and tall, her chin lifting so that her eye was fixed on one unbelievably bright and vibrant star directly ahead of her beyond the furthest Stone. She saw no people with feathered cloaks around her. No one accompanied her down the processional way. But the white light of the moon shone on her, and, beyond it, were the immeasurable stars, to remind her that life is a mystery – subtle, numinous, magnificent . . .

The Seekers, the Travellers from the West, the Guardians of the ancient stone tablet the Great Spirit had given them in trust, had come to this place in the ancient days and sang as they stared up at the black crystal eye that glinted on the white monolith. In it they saw what had been, what was and what would be in their long, long journey before they returned home. Mairi felt that this was the night for scrying: this was the night to open the secrets of Time. She stared at the black crystal. She saw her people scattered across far distant lands; she saw wars and invasions; people dying, people being born. She saw religions that demanded blood sacrifice and religions that had forgotten God. She saw men proliferating – villages growing into cities – cities turning into dust. She saw black smoke over the land so thick that the people could not breathe . . . and she saw men busy . . . always busier finding out new ways to kill each other . . .

'Where is the wisdom we were supposed to learn?' she cried. 'Where is the new wisdom we were supposed to take back to the land of our ancestors?'

She began to sob.

'There must be another future than that!' she cried. 'We have been given such gifts . . . surely . . . surely we will not waste them like that!'

'There is one gift that can yet save the future,' a voice said, a voice that she thought she recognised. It came from a long, long way away and she struggled to see who was standing against the Mark Stone beneath the Eye of Callanish. The figure was dark against the brilliance of the stone. Dazzled, her eyes stung and watered, but she persisted in trying to see who it was.

'What gift?' she cried. 'What gift?'

He stepped forward. His face was dark and kind, his robes homespun and shabby. He was Durston the hermit who believed in the gift that the Christ had brought to the earth. The new wisdom of spirit that might be put together with the old one of the Natural World before either could make sense.

Mairi shivered. The moonlight seemed to shatter into millions of slivers of silver. She fell down at his feet in a faint.

When she regained consciousness she was lying on the little

rocky knoll above the Stones. Brother Durston was on one side of her, and Neil was on the other.

She sat up and looked around her. Water flowed into Loch Roag as the tide came in. The tall Stones below them were laid out in the pattern of a Celtic cross. She had never noticed that before.

'They did not come,' she said to Neil, her voice breaking. 'They were not here, and I saw a terrible future where all the old wisdom was lost and none of the new learned.'

Durston took her hand in his.

'There is yet time, my child. Not all is lost.'

'It was so sad . . . sad . . .' she sighed, looking at the beautiful Stones standing quietly below them. The light was beginning subtly to change. It was nearly dawn.

And then she looked at Durston anxiously. 'Do you really think there is a chance? The gift that could save the future?'

He nodded. 'If we do not misuse it,' he said. 'If we have the courage to accept it.'

The eerie silver light of the moon was giving way to the gold of the sun. The eastern hills were deep purple against a sky that was at first the palest green and then suddenly the shining splendour of fire and molten gold.

The three on the hill beside the Standing Stones watched the ancient mystery of renewal, each with his own thoughts. Mairi thought of 'her people', of the greatest spirit-path of all, between the Creator and the created, which blazed like a ring of fire around the world, joining them through Time and Space with everything that lived. Durston thought of Christ in darkness on Golgotha and then rising in brilliance on the Day of Ascension to His Father who had sent Him to us as guide and pledge. Neil thought how beautiful the world was, how full of mystery and wonder, and how lucky he was to have been born to experience it.

When they returned to Kirkoway they found the villagers gathered together on the road with Sir Kenneth apparently as their leader, about to set off to look for them. As Mairi rode in on the white mare they closed menacingly in around her.

Neil had felt so elated watching the sunrise and his thoughts had reached so high, that he had forgotten that Moon-Metal was no longer Mairi's and that the Stones of Callanish were still regarded with hatred and suspicion by the rest of the community.

Sir Kenneth strode forward and confronted Mairi. He was very angry.

'Back to your old tricks again I see!' shouted Braden close behind him – his face distorted with rage as he reached up and dragged her off the mare. 'You have been to those Devil's Stones again you demon child!' he screamed, shaking her violently.

Neil moved forward quickly, but he was too late to prevent Braden's fist striking her face. As knuckle cracked against bone and Mairi cried out with the pain, Neil lost all control and flung himself forward off Flame's back and onto Braden. He could think of nothing but punching and punching that hated face. He would not at that moment have cared if he had killed him. Braden, when he had recovered from the first shock of the attack, fought back, but Neil scarcely felt the blows that fell upon himself, scarcely heard the shouting of the villagers crowding around them. He could think of nothing but smashing all opposition to Mairi, the easy way, the quick way, by brute force.

Suddenly he felt two immensely strong arms around him from behind, and he was lifted bodily off his feet and deposited roughly on the ground some way from Braden. He leapt up at once, even more fiercely, determined to continue the fight to the end. But the tall figure of Durston was between him and the man he hated. Braden, furious, turned his attack blindly on the monk. He threw punch after punch, which Thurston quietly blocked with his long, iron-hard arms, parrying every one with extraordinary skill. The crowd stopped shouting and watched as Durston stood calm, unimpassioned, rock-like while Braden exhausted himself trying to land a blow.

At last it was over. Braden drew back. Mairi and Neil, both bleeding and bruised, fell into each other's arms. Durston stood motionless – apparently not even winded.

Awed – the people had watched the confrontation silently. Now they were forced to meet the eyes of the hermit as he turned his attention to one after the other. Each one felt as though his gaze was penetrating their deepest and most secret thoughts and for the first time they confronted themselves and saw their own ignorance, their own cowardice, their own culpability. It was as though they stood before the strong and gentle Christ himself and heard him say: 'By their works shall ye know them.' Had Mairi ever done them any harm? She had helped to heal people. She had seen an angel and given them confidence that angels really existed and were near and watching over them. She had hewn wood and drawn water for her parents dutifully though her father had beaten her mercilessly. It was they who had had murderous thoughts – they who had thrown stones with the intention of killing a living human being.

One by one their eyes dropped.

When Neil had run away to Iceland with Baldur as a young boy, he had killed a man. The memory was still sickeningly fresh. On the Viking's instructions he had crept up on three men around a fire and at a signal from Baldur he had brought his axe down on one man's head with all the strength he possessed. He could still hear that terrible scream and that horrific sound of axe splitting bone. Red liquid had oozed out of the man. Red liquid dripped off his axe. He had vomited but felt no better. Where was the triumph and excitement warriors were supposed to experience when they killed? He had felt only shame and regret for what he had done, and had vowed never, never to do such a thing again. Yet – here he had been prepared to kill Braden.

Durston came to Sir Kenneth at last, but the young man did not drop his eyes as the others did. He met the hermit's eyes boldly.

'The girl stole my brother's horse,' he said defensively, 'and took it to the Devil's Stones.'

'The Devil's Stones!' Durston said bitterly. 'How many of you have been to those Stones? How many of you have seen the Devil there?'

No one answered him.

'The Devil has no need of a temple built of stone,' he said sharply. 'He can house in your hearts whenever he likes! I want you to come with me – now – and we will go to those Stones you call the Devil's Stones and see what they really are.'

'Not me! I'm not going,' Braden snarled.

'Nor I,' someone else said. 'Nor I,' a third murmured.

'Holding to old lies, I see. Afraid to face the truth?'

'Let me bury my brother,' Kenneth said suddenly, 'and then *I* will go with you, hermit.'

Fiona looked at the girl now sitting on the bank beside her brother Neil, her arm around him, wiping the blood off his face with her fingers, tenderly, caringly, forgetting her own pain. She knew she had been wrong about her. Was it not possible they were all wrong about the Stones?

'I will go too, Brother Durston,' she said.

And then one by one the villagers reluctantly agreed they would go to the Stones.

'If it will make you happier,' the hermit said, 'we will take the cross from the altar in the church and carry it before us when we go.'

'Yes . . . the cross . . . the cross . . .' the people cried and were now so eager to go to the Stones that Sir Kenneth had some trouble persuading them to stay in the village long enough to bury his brother.

After the prayers and the last sods of earth had been thrown on the grave, Durston fetched the sturdy wooden cross from the altar in the little stone church and led the people out of the village. Almost everyone had decided to come. Only the youngest children and the oldest grandparents were left behind. A long, straggling line soon developed, of silent, anxious people. They were not at all happy about going to the Stones, but now too full of curiosity to be left out of the adventure. With the holy man and the cross they hoped that they would be safe.

As the sun shone down warmly and the morning progressed many of their fears gave way to feelings of excited anticipation. Some believed that Durston was going to challenge the

Devil to single combat. As they neared the Stones the ones at the rear of the column hurried forward, anxious not to miss any of the drama.

Durston stopped when he reached the rise from which the Stones could first be seen, and waited for the stragglers to join him. Gradually they crowded in around him. There were several small ancient stone circles in the district, and a few single Standing Stones, and although all of them were avoided, none struck such fear into the hearts of the local population as the immensely tall group at Callanish.

Neil remembered wryly his first sight of them looming out of the swirling mist. Today they were white and shining in the sunlight and the Devil seemed to have no part of them. Mairi was close beside him, clinging to his arm. He could guess at some of the thoughts that must be racing through her mind.

'It is best that they see for themselves,' he whispered to her. 'It is the only way you will ever have any peace.'

She nodded, but he sensed the turmoil in her heart.

Durston turned and beckoned to her. She went to him, Neil following.

'You must have courage child.' He waved his hand at the clustering crowd. 'It is not good that they hold so stubbornly to lies.'

She nodded and bit her lip. Neil could see that she was very pale and tense.

'This is your place,' Durston said quietly to her. 'It is appropriate that you lead them in.'

Without a backward look she stepped forward. The waiting crowd gasped as she reached the Stones and did not stop, mothers clutching their children, fathers muttering.

Durston turned to face then.

'These are no Devil's Stones. You will find no evil here that you have not brought with you. The girl will show you if you let her. Follow her. Touch the stones. Enjoy the sunlight. This is a place like any other on God's earth.'

Mairi walked forward. Neil saw her straighten her back, raise her head proudly. She stepped between the first two Stones of the processional way and walked steadily forward. There was a beauty and elegance about the way she walked that surprised the people who had known her only as Braden's daughter. Neil and Durston followed her. Behind them Kenneth and Fiona, hand in hand. Gradually, one by one, the boldest stepped forward, until in the end, even the most timid had entered the avenue. At first they looked fearfully around, expecting terrible things to happen. But when nothing did happen they began to relax. Mairi stood at the centre and the others flowed around her, in and out among the Stones, chattering and laughing, pointing out a particular crystal here, a familiar island in the distant loch there. The children had left their parents and were running about shouting and laughing, jumping on the fallen Stones, playing hide and seek behind the others.

Durston and Neil stood with Mairi and looked up at the crystal Eye. In the swirling, noisy crowd, Mairi was as still as stone herself. They stood on either side of her protecting her from interruption.

Donal came up behind them. He remembered that Eye and was determined to have another look into it now that he was not alone. He took up a position and stared into it as he had before. But this time nothing happened. He shrugged and moved off.

'Nothing there,' he said cheerfully.

Braden was laughing heartily. 'The whole thing was a pack of lies!' He was holding forth gleefully to a group of his cronies. 'The girl had us all fooled. Devil – pooh!' He seemed to have forgotten that it was *he* who had claimed the Devil lived there – not his daughter.

Mairi suddenly seemed to crumple. Durston and Neil reached forwards at once and took her arms. She was weeping.

'Take her away from here,' Durston said to Neil. 'Look after her. I will speak to the others and get them home again.'

Neil led her away. He took her down the other side of the hill towards the loch. When they were far enough away they sat down side by side on a stone, his arm around her, her head on his shoulder. Her tears no longer flowed but her face was very, very sad.

'What happened?' he asked. 'Did you . . . did you see your people?'

She shook her head.

'I know I will not see them again,' she said, and Neil could hear the pain in her voice. He looked back towards the Standing Stones and knew that she was right. If they had ever been there, they would not come again. The atmosphere that had stayed undisturbed for centuries was now compromised.

They heard a shout and looked up. People were waving cheerfully at them.

'Are you coming home Mairi? We are going now.'

Neil looked quickly at Mairi. She may have lost her ancient friends, but it looked as though she now had new ones. He took her hand.

'Shall we go?'

She shrugged sadly . . . and then smiled.

'Nothing can take the memory of them away from me,' she said. 'They *were* here. They spoke to me! They will always be in my heart and I will always hold to their teaching . . .'

Neil smiled.

'The old and the new!' he said.

They could hear singing as the villagers walked off along the track towards Kirkoway.

The Stones still stood. Tall and beautiful . . . a reminder . . .

Chapter 15

The Decision

Before they reached the turn off to Kirkoway, Durston joined Mairi and Neil. He told Mairi not to be sad that her people had gone. It was inevitable that they should, and right that they should. She was strong enough now to stand alone and use what they had taught her.

'How do you mean?' Neil asked. 'What can she do? What must she do?'

Durston looked at Mairi.

'What do you think?' he asked.

Mairi looked far away into the distance for a while and Neil could feel her stillness, her composure, her new strength.

'I would like to heal the sick,' she said. 'And I would like to teach what I have learned.'

Durston smiled.

'That is a good choice,' he said, and nodded contentedly. He stretched his long limbs like a cat who has waken up from a sleep in the sun. 'I will be off now. Remember to look after her,' he said with a smile to Neil, half quizzical, half serious, and turned and walked away from them.

He did not return to Kirkoway with the others but set off towards the moors and the far mountains. Being so much with people of late had left him disturbed and restless. He longed for solitude again, the solitude that brought him nearer to his God.

It was still a good day, the sun shining, the birds singing, sometimes skimming so close to him that he could hear the whirr of their wings. Gradually as his heart calmed down and the memory of the events of the last few days stopped crowding him and took their place among the others of his long life, he prayed for Mairi and for Neil, for the young couple Fiona and Kenneth, for Donal and for all the villagers. He prayed that they would not lose the insight that they had received this day, and that they would not be so hasty to follow shadows and listen to whispers from the dark side of their hearts.

The moor was springy underfoot, the heather so deep in places that he could scarcely make headway through it, but he was determined to reach the mountains, he felt the need for a high cold mountain wind, to blow through him clearing all the clinging threads that had begun to anchor him to the world again.

He had spent long years training himself not to want the things of the world, the riches that others tricked and killed for, the comforts that made the mind lazy. He had felt the excitement of moments when 'everything made sense', when he felt momentarily so close to the mysterious 'growing point' of the spirit that it was pain to leave it, impossible to go on living without seeking it.

He believed absolutely that the world we see is only a very small part of the world that really exists and that to live only in the visible part of it is as much a waste as for a man to live in a cage hanging from a twig when he could live freely in the whole forest.

Years ago he had come to live at Uig on the headland where the great ocean thundered on the rocks below and the winds wildly blew in from the sea. There he had experienced the richness of the 'invisible' world and had used what he had learned to help, to guide, to influence . . . sometimes in the dreams of people hundreds of miles away . . . sometimes in their moments of intuition or of conscience . . . But lately he had been drawn more and more into the affairs of the people who lived on the farm near his retreat. He was becoming too attached to Neil . . . too attached to Mairi. He was losing the equilibrium so necessary for his work. Now that they no longer needed him, for his own peace of mind, he must withdraw again.

He knew that Neil would always live in the 'visible' world, but with his awareness that the other existed, and his respect for it, he would not go far wrong. Mairi herself was already marked for the greater, 'invisible' world, and she would never be satisfied with less. Whether she would choose to marry Neil, he could not tell. He hoped she would. She and Neil together would have great strength.

He decided not to return to Uig, but to stay in the mountains, to build himself a rock hut against the storms and renew his pact with the Eternal.

www.ingramcontent.com/pod-product-compliance
Lightning Source LLC
Chambersburg PA
CBHW031236260626
47169CB00007B/2322